Crider, Bill
CRIDER, BILL
ROMANTIC WAY TO DIE

11/01
2/2/02

A
ROMANTIC
WAY TO
DIE

▼

A
ROMANTIC
WAY TO
DIE

▼

A SHERIFF
DAN RHODES
MYSTERY

BILL CRIDER

THOMAS DUNNE BOOKS
ST. MARTIN'S MINOTAUR
NEW YORK

THOMAS DUNNE BOOKS.
An imprint of St. Martin's Press.

www.minotaurbooks.com

Library of Congress Cataloging-in-Publication Data

Crider, Bill.
    A romantic way to die / Bill Crider.—1st ed.
        p.   cm.—(Sheriff Dan Rhodes books)
    ISBN 0-312-20907-X
        1. Rhodes, Dan (Fictitious character)—Fiction.   2. Love stories—Authorship—Fiction.   3. Male models—Fiction.   4. Sheriffs—Fiction.   5. Texas—fiction.
    I. Title.

PS3553.R497 R66 2001
813'.54—dc21

                                                                            2001041805

First Edition: November 2001

10 9 8 7 6 5 4 3 2 1

This book is dedicated to
Earl "Speedo" Carroll
and the Cadillacs:
Thanks for the music.

A
ROMANTIC
WAY TO
DIE

▼

1

▼

THE CLEARVIEW WAL-MART WAS ALWAYS CROWDED. SOMETIMES
it seemed to Sheriff Dan Rhodes as if the Wal-Mart were, in
fact, the only store in town, and that half the population could
be found there at any given hour. Which wasn't too far from the
truth, considering that the downtown section of Clearview had
virtually disappeared over the course of the last few years. Well,
it hadn't disappeared so much as been abandoned. And then
some of the buildings had started falling down. Rhodes didn't
much like to drive through what was left of downtown these
days.

But as the downtown had crumbled, the area around the Wal-
Mart had thrived. There was a new restaurant called the Round-
Up, a new car dealership, a Sears catalog-order and appliance
store, a big grocery store, and even a McDonald's. No wonder
the parking lot was crowded.

But it was even more crowded than usual because something
special was going on, something bigger than anything that had
happened at the Wal-Mart since Elijah Ward had chained himself
to the exit door and tried to keep the customers from leaving.

That had been Ward's way of protesting the death of downtown Clearview, although it hadn't worked out quite the way Ward had planned. Before too long Ward himself had been deader than downtown, but that was another story.

The Wal-Mart was crowded today because there was a book-signing going on. The book was *Wild Texas Wind,* and the author was Ashley Leigh, better known to residents of Clearview as Vernell Lindsey, a local resident who had been trying for years to sell a romance novel and who had finally succeeded.

But although Vernell had become moderately notorious in Clearview for having written what some people considered a pretty sexy book, she was not the main attraction: Terry Don Coslin was there, too.

Terry Don had grown up in Clearview, gone away to college about ten years previously, and been discovered by a modeling agency. He had become a popular cover guy for paperback historical romances by virtue of his handsome face, his flowing locks, and his well-formed pecs, which Rhodes's wife, Ivy, had once said looked hard enough to strike a match on. Rhodes was pretty sure his own pecs weren't quite that well formed or nearly that hard.

Standing in the Wal-Mart parking lot, thinking about going inside for an autograph, Rhodes felt a little ridiculous. Not because of his inadequate pecs, and not because he hadn't read the book. He had. But he didn't feel right coming for autographs when he should have been working for the county.

Ivy had helped him rationalize it, however.

"You need to be there for crowd control," she said. "I can't get away from the office, but you can go. I can get Vernell's autograph any time, but Terry Don Coslin hasn't been back here since he graduated from high school, and he probably won't be back again. If you don't get his autograph on that book, I'm going to be really depressed."

"But we already have a copy of the book," Rhodes said. "I

wouldn't feel right, taking it in the store to get it signed."

"They wouldn't want you to, either," Ivy said. "They're there to sell new books, not to sign copies covered with reading creases. You can buy another one."

"But it costs five ninety-nine."

"So?"

Ivy had a way of saying "So?" that precluded arguments, so Rhodes agreed to buy another copy of the book. And to engage in crowd control if need be.

The crowd was certainly there. There were cars, pickups, and SUVs parked in every available space in the Wal-Mart parking lot, and in the grocery store lot as well. They were parked along the shoulder of the road and in the fire lane. They were parked wherever there was a space big enough to hold them. And sometimes where there wasn't.

Rhodes didn't even consider writing any parking tickets. In the first place, he'd never written a parking ticket before, and he wasn't ready to start. And in the second place, he didn't want to start an anti-law-enforcement riot because, in the third place, his own car was illegally parked. So he ignored all the parking violations and started walking toward the store entrance.

He hadn't gone far when he passed two women who were standing beside an SUV that towered over both of them. They were talking about *Wild Texas Wind,* and about Terry Don Coslin.

"I didn't think Vernell knew anything about sex," one of the women said. She was tall and lanky and wore Levi's and a checked western-style shirt. "But that book's pretty hot."

The other woman was neither tall nor lanky. She had on a faded blue sweat suit that she'd probably bought at Wal-Mart a year or so previously and washed two or three times a week ever since.

"I don't know about Vernell," she said. "But I'll bet you Terry Don Coslin does."

Both women noticed Rhodes at that moment and laughed self-consciously. Rhodes pretended he hadn't heard them. He already knew who the main attraction at the signing was, and he was willing to bet there wasn't a single male in the line to get an inscription, not unless the male had been sent there by his wife, as Rhodes had been.

The crowd inside the store was even larger than Rhodes had expected. Most of the cars, pickups, and SUVs outside must've been carrying two or three people at least. There was hardly room to move once Rhodes got inside the doors. The harassed greeter tried to wave at Rhodes over the heads of the mob, but there was a sudden surge and she disappeared completely. The manager had long since given up trying to maintain order, and Rhodes wondered if maybe Ivy hadn't been right about the need for crowd control.

A large woman clutching a copy of *Wild Texas Wind* bumped into Rhodes, shoving him to one side. At that moment, he decided that for once in his life he was going to use his badge to his own advantage.

"Sheriff coming through," he said over and over as he elbowed his way through the buzzing swarm.

Before long he had reached the signing table, receiving only minor scratches and abrasions along the way.

"Hey, Vernell," he said when he got to the table, which was set up on an elevated platform.

Vernell pushed back her long hair and looked up from the book she was signing. She wore a harried look and an outfit that Rhodes thought he recognized. It consisted of an off-shoulder shirt with several buttons undone and a long skirt that was slit most of the way up to the waist. It was almost identical to the outfit worn by the female model on the cover of Vernell's book.

Vernell's appearance had definitely changed, Rhodes thought. She usually dressed in a conventionally buttoned shirt and old jeans. Her hair was generally caught up and held in the back with a big plastic clip. Rhodes decided that authors would do anything for publicity, not that there was anything wrong with her new image.

"Hey, Sheriff," Vernell said.

That was all she had time for. She looked back down and scrawled something in the book a woman was holding open in front of her.

Terry Don Coslin hadn't even noticed Rhodes yet. He was completely surrounded by women, one of whom was sitting on the signing table. Rhodes was relieved to see that he was fully clothed. After his glance at Vernell, Rhodes had momentarily feared that Terry Don's steel pecs might be in view.

Terry Don in person was imposing enough, even with his short-sleeved shirt on. He obviously either worked out a lot or was one of those truly fortunate humans who was born with the genes of a natural hunk. His biceps bulged impressively, and the shirt strained so at the shoulders that Rhodes thought it might rip apart all the way down the back at any moment.

If that happened, it would be all over. No amount of crowd control in the world could prevent the women from mobbing the table and carrying Terry Don away for private ravishment. Either that, or they'd tear him apart in the struggle. Rhodes didn't even like to think about it.

Rhodes picked up a copy of *Wild Texas Wind* from the stack in front of Vernell and opened it to the title page. He waited until a red-faced woman who appeared near to weeping (she had just gotten Terry Don's signature and a few kind words into the bargain) got her book back from Vernell. Then Rhodes put his copy down on the table.

"Could you sign that for Ivy, please?" he said.

"I'd be glad to," Vernell said.

"You're selling a ton of books," Rhodes said as she wrote.

She finished writing and closed the book.

"You know something?" she said. "I really am. But it's not really the book they're interested in."

Rhodes nodded toward Terry Don.

"That's right," Vernell said. "When the book first came out, I did a signing here. I sold three copies, and one of those was to my cousin."

"Helps to have good pecs," Rhodes said.

"You can say that again."

Rhodes decided not to.

"I don't mind, though," Vernell said. "I'm getting a royalty on every copy, and all the publicity will be a real boost for the conference."

The conference was something that Vernell had been working on ever since her book had sold. It was a weekend retreat for romance writers to be held at the old college campus at Obert, a little town about eight miles from Clearview. The campus had been deserted for years, but it had finally been restored to something vaguely resembling its former glory and was now open for business, in a manner of speaking. It offered weekend retreats for church groups and businesses, and now it was hosting a writers' conference.

"I'm sure the conference will be a big success," Rhodes said as Vernell handed him his book.

Vernell nodded, already signing someone else's copy, and Rhodes turned to Terry Don, insinuating himself in front of two women who were crowding close to the table.

He put his book down and said, "Could you sign this for me?"

Terry Don looked up. He had very blue eyes, which Rhodes had to admit looked good with his dark hair, hair that was even longer than Vernell's.

Rhodes hadn't known Terry Don when he'd lived in Clearview. He remembered having seen him play football for the Clearview Catamounts a couple of times, though. He'd been a wide receiver, and a pretty good one. He'd been all-district his senior year.

"I'd be glad to sign it," Terry Don said. "Is it for you?"

"It's for my wife," Rhodes said. "Her name's Ivy."

Terry Don smiled. His teeth were very white and very straight.

"That's a nice, old-fashioned name," he said.

The women behind Rhodes were jostling him, impatient for their turn with Terry Don.

"She's a nice woman," Rhodes said. "She liked your picture."

Terry Don shrugged. "It's a living."

He signed the book and handed it to Rhodes. Rhodes took it and worked his way back through the women straining to get closer to Terry Don.

When he was nearly to the express check-out lane, Rhodes looked back. Terry Don glanced up and grinned at him over the heads of the crowd. He was clearly having a good time, enjoying the feeling of being famous in his old hometown. Rhodes could see that it was more than just a job to Terry Don. Terry Don was having fun.

2

▼

AFTER A TOO-LONG WAIT IN LINE, RHODES PAID FOR HIS BOOK (glad to get the Wal-Mart discount), left the store, and drove to the Blacklin County Jail, which resembled something left over from the nineteenth century with its red, rough, weathered stone walls and barred windows. But it looked much older than it actually was. It had been built in the 1920s, rather than the 1820s, but even at that it was one of the older jails currently in use in the state. Many other counties had built spanking-new "law enforcement centers" that were chock-full of all sorts of helpful new gadgets the Blacklin County commissioners had decided that their law officers didn't really need at the present time. They pointed out happily that the jail had passed its last inspection by the state, and that was good enough for them.

It was good enough for Rhodes, too, since he didn't have much faith in gadgets. The prisoners hadn't suffered any particular deprivation that he was aware of, not unless you counted the fact that they didn't have satellite TV or that they'd recently been terrorized by a ghost. But the ghost was gone now, unofficially exorcized by Rhodes, and things were pretty much back to normal, or what passed for normal in the Blacklin County Jail.

Rhodes went inside, and Hack Jensen, the dispatcher, looked up. Then he looked over at Lawton, the jailer, who was dusting off Rhodes's desk. Lawton stopped dusting and watched Hack expectantly, which Rhodes knew was a bad sign. Something was going on, and if things went the way they usually did, it would take him a lot longer than it should have to get the whole story out of the two of them. They got an unseemly pleasure out of making him extract the information from them bit by bit, and the longer they could drag out the process, the better they liked it.

"Glad you could make it in today, Sheriff," Hack said.

The dispatcher was tall and thin and wore a narrow moustache that was nearly completely gray. He reminded Rhodes of Bud Abbott, whom Rhodes had seen only in the old black-and-white movies in which he teamed up with Lou Costello, to whom, by a pleasant coincidence, Lawton bore a chubby resemblance. The significance of the resemblance wasn't lost on Rhodes, who sometimes thought that Hack and Lawton would have made a great team if vaudeville hadn't died.

"Yeah, Sheriff," Lawton said, grinning. "Glad to see you."

Rhodes went over to his desk, and Lawton moved away so Rhodes could sit down.

"What's been going on?" Rhodes said, more to set things in motion than in any expectation of an actual answer. "No more ghosts, I hope."

Hack looked thoughtful. "Could be a ghost, I guess. What do you think, Lawton?"

Lawton shook his head. "Nope. Couldn't be a ghost. Ghosts can't use telephones." He scratched his head. "Or can they?"

Hack looked chagrined, and Rhodes knew why. Lawton had made a rookie mistake and, without intending to, had revealed that the problem, whatever it was, involved telephones. Hack had probably been counting on keeping that information back for at least another five minutes.

Rhodes pressed his advantage and took what he hoped was a logical guess.

"Have there been any prank calls I should know about?"

Hack gave Lawton a look that could have peeled three coats of varnish off an oak armoire.

Lawton hung his head.

"Dang," he said.

Rhodes didn't smile. It wouldn't do to have them thinking he felt as if he'd won. They'd both sulk all day if that happened.

"I thought I'd heard something about that," he said, giving them an out to save their pride.

"Who told you?" Lawton asked, relieved to be off the hook. "It was Pearl Taylor, I'll bet. Where'd you see her?"

"I've been out at the Wal-Mart," Rhodes said. "Checking out the size of the crowd at the book signing."

That was more or less true, and Rhodes was hoping that Lawton wouldn't notice he hadn't mentioned seeing Pearl Taylor or anyone else.

"That Pearl," Lawton said. "I guess she had to go out there and see Terry Don Coslin, just like nearly ever'body in town."

"Ever'body but us," Hack said. "We didn't get to go, not even when there's a big celebrity in town. Somebody has to stay here and see to the jail and the prisoners and be sure the calls get answered. That's the way it always is. We work hard and keep the county goin', but we never seem to get in on the excitement."

"Boy, you got that right," Lawton said. "I guess the last time we got in on anything was the ghost, and that was because he was right here in the jail. If it was something we had to go out and see, we'd just be left out like we always are."

Rhodes knew that he had to cut them off. If they got started on that theme, they could go on for hours.

"About those phone calls," he said.

"Who else was out there at Wal-Mart?" Hack asked. "What did they have to say?"

Rhodes wasn't going to get caught that easily.

"I'd rather hear what the callers told you," he said. "You know how it is when you're in a crowd. Sometimes people talk just to let everyone else hear them, and it's hard to get a straight story."

"Yeah," Lawton said. "Pearl Taylor's like that. There never was a woman liked to talk as much as she does. I thought Hack wasn't ever gonna get her off the line."

"She wasn't the prank caller, though," Rhodes said, pretty sure that he was safe in saying so. Pearl liked to talk, all right, but she wasn't widely known for her sense of humor.

"Nope," Hack said. "She was the one got the call. And she wasn't the only one." He checked his computer log. "We've already had three other calls about that contest."

Rhodes almost made the mistake of asking what contest Hack was talking about, but he caught himself in time. Instead he asked who else had called.

"Rose Gentry, Martha Rutherford, and Henrietta Bayam," Hack said. "They all got calls saying they'd won."

" 'Course they'd already called the radio station," Lawton said. "That's why they called here."

Hack glared at him. It was Hack's job to tell the story. Lawton was just supposed to help him string Rhodes along. And now Lawton had made another mistake and revealed that the radio station was somehow involved.

"K-Vue?" Rhodes asked, using the station's nickname, which was based on the station's way of pronouncing the call letters KVUE.

"You know of any other radio stations in town?" Hack asked. "Or the county, for that matter?"

Rhodes admitted he didn't know of any.

"Wait a second," Lawton said, looking suspicious. "Didn't Pearl tell you about the radio station?"

Rhodes shook his head. "I don't think she said a thing about it."

"Well, she should've," Hack said. "She wanted to blame the station at first. So did the others. It sounded like a real contest to all of 'em."

Rhodes was beginning to get the picture.

"Pearl didn't tell me what she was supposed to have won," he said.

"She was prob'ly too excited at seein' Terry Don in person," Hack said. "That was what the contest was all about, more or less."

Rhodes thought he had just about all the pieces to the puzzle now.

"Somebody who was supposed to be from the radio station called Pearl and those others to tell them they'd won a date with Terry Don Coslin," he said.

"Yeah," Hack said. "And those women were pretty upset when they found out it wasn't the truth, let me tell you."

"They would've known there wasn't any contest if they'd listened to the radio," Lawton said. "There hasn't been a word about it on the air."

Rhodes looked at the little TV set on Hack's desk. It was tuned in to *The Young and the Restless*. The sound was turned off, but Rhodes could see a man wearing a moustache and a serious expression. He was deep in conversation with a blond woman.

"We listen to the radio now and then," Lawton said defensively. "Which you'd know if you stayed around here more. It's about the only way to get any news in this place, since we don't ever get to go out. Not that there's been a good reporter at that station since Red Rogers got killed."

"I sort of miss old Red," Hack said. "Even if he was a bee in the sheriff's bonnet."

"Let's get back to the contest," Rhodes said. "Did any of those women recognize the voice of the person who called them?"

"Nope," Hack said. "They couldn't even tell if it was a man or a woman. Just said it was a nice voice, kinda soft, but not too soft. Kinda low, but not too low. When they called the K-Vue, they got the word that nobody from there had called them. That's when they called here."

"Sounds to me like somebody tryin' to make trouble for Vernell and that writers' conference she's havin'," Lawton said. "Why anybody'd want to do that beats me. It's good publicity for the whole county. There was even somethin' about it on the news out of Dallas last night."

Rhodes hadn't seen the news, but he knew that Vernell's conference had been getting a lot of attention. She'd managed to get several fairly well known writers of historical romances to take part, and she'd also landed Jeanne Arnot, a New York agent who'd sold so many books, including Vernell's, to so many different publishers that she was called the "Queen of Love." And of course there was the star attraction: Terry Don Coslin.

"Somebody's got it in for Vernell, that's for sure," Hack said. "Or maybe for the radio station. Find out who it is, and you'll find out who's been makin' those calls."

"I'll see what I can do," Rhodes said, though he really didn't think there was any way to find out who the caller had been. "Don't any of those women have caller ID?"

"Blocked," Hack said.

"What about that call-back deal? Star six-nine."

"Blocked that, too."

"It figures," Rhodes said.

As soon as someone came up with something that might be helpful to law enforcement, someone else found out a way around it. In his more pessimistic moments, Rhodes suspected that it was all part of a conspiracy by the phone company. First they sold you the caller ID. Then they sold people a way to block it. Then they found a way to keep your phone from accepting blocked calls and sold you that. Next they'd be advertising a way to get blocked calls through whatever was keeping them out. And then . . . he didn't even want to think about it. Besides, there wasn't just a single phone company now. There were lots of phone companies. So there couldn't be any conspiracy.

"What's Deputy Grady working on?" he asked, to change the subject.

"She's down in Thurston," Hack said. "Somebody broke into an antique store down there last night. I don't think they took any antiques, but there was some money in the cash register. They got that."

"Kids, most likely," Lawton said. "Didn't know what an antique was."

"Any vandalism?" Rhodes asked.

"Not to speak of," Hack told him. "Not unless you count the broken window."

"I don't think I will," Rhodes said. "Count it, I mean."

"If Pearl Taylor calls back, can I tell her you're on the case?"

"You do that," Rhodes said.

But he didn't really have any intention of doing anything. Prank callers were almost impossible to catch, and it all seemed harmless enough. It was irritating to the women who had been called, but it wasn't exactly a major crime. Instead of worrying about it, he sat at his desk, put on his glasses, and got busy with his paperwork.

3
▼

THE REST OF THE DAY WAS FULL OF THE USUAL KINDS OF things that a sheriff's office in a small county had to deal with. Nothing exciting, but time-consuming nevertheless: cows wandering loose on county roads and posing a danger to the traffic, drivers running into ditches or into the loose cattle or through someone's fence, neighbors getting into loud arguments over pets or property lines, a possibly rabid possum terrorizing homeowners just outside of town, calls saying that someone had been shooting at mailboxes and road signs out near the Milsby community.

Rhodes didn't have to deal with any of those things himself. Ruth Grady or Buddy Reynolds responded to the calls and calmed the callers, tried to find the owners of the livestock, put a stop to the arguments, and trapped the possum, which was to be held for observation by Dr. Slick, one of the local vets. The possum didn't look rabid to Rhodes, but then he didn't know much about that kind of thing, and it was always a good idea to be careful.

When he got home that evening, Ivy was already there. The

first thing she said when he walked through the door was, "Did you get my book?"

Rhodes brought his hand from behind his back and showed her the book.

"Signed by Terry Don Coslin himself," he said. "Get away, Yancey."

Yancey was Rhodes's Pomeranian, and his one talent was barking. That, and circling around Rhodes's ankles trying to take a nip at them.

"He's just excited to see you," Ivy said.

Yancey continued barking, circling, and nipping. Rhodes sighed and handed the book to Ivy, who opened it to see what Terry Don and Vernell had written.

"Did you read this inscription?" Ivy asked.

Rhodes hadn't. He hadn't even thought about reading it. He nudged Yancey aside with one foot and moved to look over Ivy's shoulder.

Vernell had written "To Ivy with all best wishes" above her signature.

Terry Don had written "To Ivy, the woman with the nice name."

"Wasn't that sweet?" Ivy said.

Rhodes said he guessed it was.

"You're not jealous, are you?" Ivy asked. "Because he's not a threat to you."

"Are you sure? He's got muscles you wouldn't believe."

Ivy closed the book and looked at the cover.

"I believe," she said.

Rhodes nudged Yancey away with his foot. Yancey kept yapping.

"I think I'd better feed Speedo," Rhodes said. "Give you a little time alone with Terry Don."

Ivy hit him in the shoulder, but she didn't try to stop him. He went out into the back yard to get Speedo's dish. Yancey bounded out the door behind him. Besides barking and nipping at Rhodes, Yancey liked barking and running around with Speedo, who was at least partially a border collie and considerably larger than Yancey, who pretended not to notice the difference. Or maybe he really didn't notice, Rhodes thought. Brain power wasn't one of Yancey's assets.

It was a cool fall evening, and Rhodes could see the first stars beginning to appear through the bare branches of the pecan trees whose leaves covered the ground. Rhodes wasn't fond of raking leaves, and they didn't seem to bother Speedo, whose real name was Mr. Earl and who bounded around the yard with Yancey yipping and nipping along behind.

Rhodes filled Speedo's bowl with Old Roy dog food and stood for a minute, enjoying the evening and the dogs. Then he called Yancey and went back inside, looking forward to a quiet evening at home.

Supper was chili, made with extra lean beef, which Rhodes insisted on eating with beans, a habit that would have disgusted any chili purists who caught him at it. Rhodes didn't care. He liked beans in his chili, and he didn't think any chili purists were likely to happen by.

While they ate, he and Ivy discussed the writers' conference. Yancey had finally settled down and gone to sleep so that it was quiet enough for talking.

"I wouldn't mind going to that conference, myself," Ivy said. "Except that I'm not a writer."

"What will they be doing?" Rhodes asked, having no idea of what went on at a writers' conference.

"They'll talk about writing," Ivy said. "Vernell has some really well-known people on the program."

"And people come to listen to them?"

"Lots of people," Ivy said. "Vernell filled every spot she had.

She could have sold more places, but there just wasn't room."

Rhodes crumbled some crackers into his chili and said that he didn't know so many people wanted to be romance writers.

"You'd be surprised," Ivy said. "I'll bet there are twenty women in Clearview with manuscripts stuck away somewhere. Maybe more than that. Everybody wants to write a book."

"I don't," Rhodes said.

"You're the exception, then."

"You mean you want to write one?"

Ivy shook her head and laughed. "No, not me. I'm an exception, too. I just like reading them."

"But you said you wouldn't mind going to the conference."

"That's because I'd like to meet the writers. Marian Willoughby will be there, and Serena Thayer. Belinda Marshall, too."

Rhodes spooned chili into his mouth and said nothing. He'd never read a book by any of the women Ivy had mentioned. He'd read Vernell's book only because she lived in Clearview and was a friend of Ivy's.

It wasn't that he didn't like to read. It was just that he rarely had time, and when he did have a spare moment, he was happier watching a bad old movie than reading a book.

"And Terry Don Coslin will be there, too," Rhodes said. "Don't forget Terry Don."

"I'm not interested in him at all," Ivy said.

"I don't blame you. Not when you have a guy like me around the house."

"Right."

"So you're only interested in the writers."

"Of course. I think writers must be fascinating people."

"Probably not much different from anyone else," Rhodes said.

"I'd think they have better imaginations."

"Speaking of imagination," Rhodes said, "somebody in this town sure has one."

He told her about the "contest." When he was done, he asked if she could think of anyone who might have a grudge against Vernell. Or against the radio station, for that matter.

"I'd think nearly everyone in town would have a grudge against that station," Ivy said. "The music they play is pretty bad."

Rhodes had to agree. About a year previously, KVUE had switched to the "Young Country" format, which meant that no song over five minutes old was ever played, and no performer over the age of thirty got any airtime. That meant that no performer Rhodes had ever heard of got played, except the Dixie Chicks. There was nothing wrong with the Dixie Chicks.

"I can't go after everyone in town," Rhodes said. "That's too many suspects. What about people with a grudge against Vernell?"

"I can't think of anyone, except maybe Henrietta Bayam."

Henrietta had been one of those who called to complain, but that didn't mean anything. She might have called to avert suspicion.

"What about Henrietta?" Rhodes asked.

"There was quite a bit of gossip about her and Vernell. Are you sure you haven't heard?"

Rhodes pushed away his empty chili bowl.

"I'm sure," he said.

Ivy took a sip of water and set her glass back on the table.

"Henrietta told a few people that Vernell stole the idea for *Wild Texas Wind* from her."

"How could she do that?" Rhodes asked.

"They were in a writers' group, and—"

"Hold it. What's a writers' group?"

"People get together and read chapters of their books to each other. That way they get feedback and criticism."

Rhodes couldn't imagine people sitting around and reading chapters of unsold books to each other, so he found it hard to believe that there was a writers' group in Clearview. Ivy assured him that there was.

"In fact," she said, "there are two. One for romance writers and one for mystery writers. Your friend Clyde Ballinger is in that one."

Rhodes knew that Ballinger had an excessive fondness for old paperbacks with titles like *Bargain in Blood* and *A Touch of Death* and *The Jugger,* but he'd had no idea that Ballinger aspired to write a book like the ones he read.

"I told you," Ivy said. "Everyone wants to write a book. The people who aren't writing romance novels are writing mysteries."

"It must pay awfully well," Rhodes said.

"I don't have any idea."

"It doesn't matter. So Henrietta must've thought Vernell stole her idea from something that she read at one of those group meetings."

"That's it," Ivy said. "I don't think Henrietta has spoken to Vernell since the book was published."

"I wonder if Henrietta's going to the writers' conference," Rhodes said.

Ivy didn't know. "You could call her and ask if you really want to know."

Rhodes didn't want to call Henrietta. He thought it was silly to have made the prank calls, but he wasn't really interested in finding out who'd done it. What harm could a few calls do?

"You couldn't call Henrietta, anyway," Ivy said. "I just remembered. She wouldn't be at home if she went to the conference. The programs started tonight, and everyone's staying out there at the college."

"Why not just come back to town after the meetings and sleep in your own bed?" Rhodes asked.

"That way you'd miss out on all the association with the writers."

"Oh," Rhodes said.

He decided to forget about the prank calls.

"Are there any good movies on tonight?" he asked.

"If you'll help me clean up the dishes," Ivy said, "I'll tell you."

It turned out that there was a good movie on, one of Rhodes's favorite westerns, *The Comancheros,* and he finished helping Ivy just in time for them to get in on the beginning. After John Wayne had ridden off into the sunset, with Stuart Whitman and Ina Balin waving good-bye, Rhodes and Ivy went to bed.

"Just think," Ivy said as she lay back on her pillow. "All those women out there in Obert have to settle for sleeping in the same building with Terry Don Coslin, but I have you."

"I'm glad you appreciate me," Rhodes said.

Ivy grinned. "You bet I do," she said.

Rhodes dreamed that he was a rugged frontiersman who wore fringed leather pants but no shirt. His pecs were hard as oak, and his flat, ridged stomach was equally hard. He was racing along astride a straining stallion, in hot pursuit of a woman whose long hair streamed out behind her as she galloped ahead of him. She looked a little like Ina Balin would have looked in *The Comancheros* if she'd taken her hair down.

He was just about to catch her when the telephone woke him.

"You better get out to Obert quick," Hack said when Rhodes managed to answer. "We got big trouble."

"How big?" Rhodes asked.

"Henrietta Bayam's dead. And there's a naked woman runnin' around loose."

"I'm already on the way," Rhodes said.

4
▼

THE COLLEGE CAMPUS AT OBERT SAT ON THE TOP OF OBERT'S hill. The hill was the highest point between Houston and Dallas, which was why Obert had at one time been considered as a possible location of the Texas state capital. Austin had won out, however, and Obert had sunk into an extended period of obscurity, its only claim to fame being the small private college, which had been founded shortly after the Civil War and had struggled along under the management of one denomination or other for nearly a hundred years before closing its doors forever in the early 1960s.

The campus had decayed steadily for a long time after that, until it had been bought by a rare-book dealer named Simon Graham, who planned to restore it and use it as a place to hold conferences and meetings. Graham's plans had been brought to a sudden halt by his murder, and it seemed that the campus would continue its decline. But then Tom Chatterton, a wealthy antiques dealer from Dallas, had bought it and finished the restoration work.

The old main building was the only original building left on the site, but other buildings had been added over the years of the college's life. These included a dormitory, a gymnasium, and a home that had been the president's residence. Graham had managed to restore only the latter building before his murder, but Chatterton had seen the project through to the end. The main building, the dormitory, and the gym had been set to rights at considerable expense, and the campus was now open for business for the first time in nearly forty years.

Vernell's conference was just the first of many that Chatterton hoped to host on his rejuvenated property, and he was in charge of all the arrangements. Vernell had worked closely with him, and it was really his conference as much as it was hers.

Things hadn't gotten off to a rousing start, Rhodes thought as he drove around the wide curve that led through the heart of Obert (a post office, a combination barbershop/feedstore, and several deserted buildings) to the old campus.

As best as Rhodes could understand the story from Hack, whom Rhodes had called again once he got dressed, there had been a noisy fight in one of the dormitory rooms after the conference had shut down for the night. The door to the room was closed when people got there, and it was quiet inside. No one had wanted to open the door, but someone finally had, and they found Henrietta lying on the floor.

"I'd barely got the phone hung up from that one," Hack told Rhodes, "when it rang again. I didn't even have time to call you."

"What was the second call?" Rhodes asked.

"That was the one about the naked woman. It was Miz Appleby that called. You remember her?"

Rhodes was acquainted with all the Applebys, including the abusive husband, Cy, who was now a resident at one of the state's penitentiary units, thanks to Rhodes. Rhodes thought that

Cy's imprisonment had done his family a world of good. Besides his wife, there was a daughter, Twyla Faye, and twin sons, Claude and Clyde.

"I remember Mrs. Appleby," Rhodes said. "Why did she call?"

"Well, she's the one who saw the naked woman. Miz Appleby was gettin' a breath of air when she saw something in her yard. It was pretty dark, but Miz Appleby said there was enough of a moon for her to tell it was a woman runnin' by, not wearin' a stitch."

Rhodes pulled up in front of the dormitory, a long, one-story wooden structure that sat to one side of the old main building, which was silhouetted against the night sky like the castle in a black-and-white Frankenstein movie.

All the lights were on in the dormitory, and when Rhodes got out of the county car, a man came out of the dorm to meet him. The man was short, bald, and had a neatly trimmed white beard. He was wearing a khaki shirt and khaki cargo pants. Rhodes had never seen him in person, but he'd seen his picture in the Clearview newspaper.

"I'm Tom Chatterton," the man said, extending his hand. "No relation to the English poet."

Rhodes wasn't sure what that meant. English poets hadn't been his strong point in school. He shook hands and introduced himself.

"Everyone's a little distracted in there," Chatterton said with a glance over his shoulder.

Sudden death had a way of distracting people, Rhodes thought.

"What happened?" he asked.

"Well, I don't really know. There's a woman in one of the rooms, and she's dead. I do know that much. I don't know what happened to her."

Rhodes thought about the naked woman that Mrs. Appleby had seen.

"What about everyone else?" he asked. "All present and accounted for?"

"I believe so," Chatterton said. He seemed a little distracted himself. "Why don't you come inside and see what you can find out."

"I need to see the body first," Rhodes said. "Is there a back door?"

"Yes," Chatterton said, and led the way around the side of the dormitory.

The grass was damp, and Rhodes could feel the chilly dew clinging to the bottom of his pants legs as they brushed against his socks. The yellow light from the dormitory windows threw yellow rectangles across the dark ground.

The back door was locked, but Chatterton had a key.

"Is this door always locked?" Rhodes asked.

"Yes, but it's easily opened from the inside in case of fire," Chatterton said, as if Rhodes might be there on a routine fire safety inspection.

They went inside into a narrow hallway. Henrietta's room was the last one at the end of the hall.

"Right here," Chatterton said, pushing open the door.

The room was small, with two single beds, not much more than cots, really, and a little dresser with a mirror hanging above it. The mirror was slightly askew, and one drawer of the dresser was open about a quarter of an inch. The door to a tiny closet stood open, and Rhodes could see clothes hanging inside.

He looked over at the window screen. It was crooked, as if it had been opened and carelessly shut.

Henrietta Bayam was lying on the floor. Her head was near the dresser, and her neck was turned at an odd angle. There was a small pool of blood under her head. Rhodes stepped into the room and bent down over Henrietta. There was no question in his mind that she was dead, but he felt for a pulse nevertheless. There was none, of course. Henrietta's flesh felt only slightly cool to his touch.

Rhodes stood up and sighed.

"Let's go back around to the front," Rhodes said. "I have a few calls to make before I talk to anyone else."

He and Chatterton walked back through the clammy grass and crossed the yellow rectangles.

"It won't take long," Rhodes said when they reached the front. "You can just wait here."

Chatterton stood outside the dormitory while Rhodes got Hack on the radio and asked him to send out Ruth Grady to do a crime-scene investigation of the room.

"Send the justice of the peace, too," he said. "I'll have Ruth call for the ambulance later."

"Ten-four," Hack said.

Rhodes got out of the car and walked over to where Chatterton was waiting patiently.

"All right," he said. "Let's go in."

Chatterton didn't say a word, just turned and went back into the dormitory. Rhodes followed him.

As soon as they got inside, Rhodes knew what Chatterton had meant about distraction. There were at least thirty women crammed into the dormitory's sitting room. Some of them were dressed, some of them were half-dressed, and some of them were wearing robes. All of them were talking at once. Rhodes had no idea how any of them could make out what the others were saying. He certainly couldn't.

He looked at Chatterton, who shrugged, raised his eyebrows, and held up his palms.

Rhodes wished he had a police whistle, but he'd never needed one before and didn't carry one around. He thought for a second that he might have to fire his pistol to get their attention, but it turned out not to be necessary. Someone else was better equipped for the situation than Rhodes was.

There was a shrill, piercing blast, and the room got quiet immediately. Rhodes looked to the side of the room to see a very short woman, shorter than Chatterton, putting a police whistle on a silver chain back into her purse.

"I always carry one," she said in a New York kind of voice. "You never know when you'll need help, and they're good for hailing taxis."

"And you are?" Rhodes said.

"Jeanne Arnot. And you?"

"I'm the sheriff. Dan Rhodes."

"Where's your badge?"

Rhodes always wore civilian clothes, and his badge was clipped to his belt. He pulled it off and held it up so that everyone could see it.

"Well, it's about time you got here," Jeanne said. "New York's finest would have been on the scene in under five minutes."

"He had to come from Clearview," Vernell Lindsey said in Rhodes's defense. "It's a long way."

Vernell was wearing a pink robe and pink slippers. In fact, Rhodes noticed, pink was the dominant theme in sleeping attire for the entire crowd. Jeanne Arnot was wearing gray slacks, but she had on a pink blouse, and two women wore pink dresses. One woman had on fuzzy pink bunny slippers. Rhodes couldn't remember having seen anything quite like them.

"Long way or not, there's a dead woman in that room back there," Jeanne said, and by the time she'd finished the sentence everyone in the room was talking again.

Some were talking to Rhodes, some were talking to each other, and some were just talking to keep from being the only ones who weren't talking. Rhodes held up his hands for quiet, but he didn't get it. He was thinking of his pistol again when the shrill of the whistle cut the air.

"I never heard such a bunch of hens cackling," Jeanne said into the sudden silence.

Though he'd been thinking along the same lines, Rhodes was glad she'd been the one to say it. If a man had made a crack like that, he'd have been in big trouble.

"Keep it down and let the sheriff do his job," Jeanne went on. "This is not a time for yakking."

There was no response, and Jeanne said, "It's all yours, Sheriff."

"Thanks," Rhodes said. "Let's take this one step at a time. Who can tell me what happened?"

Chatterton raised his hand. "I can. Or at least I think I can."

"Fine," Rhodes said. "Why don't you give it a try."

5

▼

ACCORDING TO CHATTERTON, THE EVENING HAD GONE ALONG just fine, at least at the beginning. Most of the conference participants had arrived at the campus between noon and five o'clock, and around seven they'd had dinner in the main building.

"There's a nice room on the first floor that I had converted to a dining room," Chatterton said. "The dinner was catered by the Round-Up, and—"

"And there was no vegetarian plate!" a woman said loudly.

"I've already apologized for that," Chatterton said. "The Round-Up's management doesn't exactly understand vegetarians, but there will be something for everyone from now on, I assure you."

"There'd better be," the woman said, clearly quite angry.

She was a willowy blonde with startling blue eyes. She wore a dark green robe, and Rhodes was sure she'd put on makeup before coming into the sitting room, or else hadn't yet taken it off. Rhodes wondered what kind of person worried more about what she ate and how she looked than about some dead woman in another room of the same building.

"Never fear," Chatterton told the blonde in a placating tone. "At any rate, Sheriff, after dinner we had our first general session, sort of a welcome aboard, and then Ms. Arnot gave us some insights into the kind of books she's looking for at her agency."

"Good ones," Jeanne said. "That's what we're looking for."

"Yes," Chatterton said. "After that, some people had appointments with Ms. Arnot to discuss their manuscripts. Everyone else was free to mingle and talk either in the dormitory rooms or in the main building. There's no television here. I believe in the value of reading and conversation."

Rhodes was sure that was commendable, and he felt a little guilty for having watched *The Comancheros* instead of reading a few chapters of *David Copperfield*.

But he had other things to worry about, like where everyone had been when the commotion had started. It took him a while to get it all sorted out. Jeanne Arnot had been in the main building, meeting with prospective clients one after the other at thirty-minute intervals, and though the meetings had been over before the disturbance began, she had remained in the main building.

"Because there's no smoking in here," she said. "Can you believe that? I could use a cigarette right now."

Rhodes said he didn't make the rules and asked who else was in the main building.

"Serena was there," Jeanne said. "She might be a vegan, but she doesn't mind if I smoke."

"That's because you got so much money for her last book," someone said, and Jeanne laughed.

"You could be right. How about it, Serena?"

The willowy blonde smiled enigmatically and said, "Anything's possible, Jeanne."

"With you, I'd say that was an understatement. Anyway, she's the only one I can vouch for, Sheriff, but that's just because I don't know many of the others. There were still quite a few people there."

"What about here?" Rhodes asked. "Who was in the dormitory?"

"I was," Chatterton said. "I was checking to make sure everything was all right and that everyone had everything she needed before I went to the president's house for the night. That's when the screaming started."

"It wasn't screaming, exactly," Vernell said. "I was here, too, Sheriff, in my room, with Carrie Logan. We were getting ready for bed. Isn't that right, Carrie?"

Rhodes recognized Carrie, who worked at the Clearview post office. She was tall and heavy and one of the most efficient people behind the counter. Rhodes would never have guessed that she was a romance writer.

"That's right," Carrie said.

Her voice was a little shaky, as if she might be nervous. If she was, Rhodes didn't blame her.

"We were just about to go to bed when we heard Henrietta," Carrie went on, her voice getting stronger. "It was more like yelling than screaming."

"Did you notice what time it was?" Rhodes asked.

"It was just about eleven-thirty," Carrie said. "I have this little travel clock that I brought with me, and it was on the dresser."

"How do you know it was Henrietta who yelled?" Rhodes asked.

"Well, she's the one who was lying on the floor when we looked in," Carrie said.

"And that's when the real screaming started," someone else put in.

Carrie said, "You walk in on a dead woman that you've seen two or three times a week for the last ten years, and you'd scream, too."

"Who was sharing the room with Henrietta?" Rhodes asked.

"That would be me, Sheriff," Lorene Winslow said.

Lorene was a teller at the First Union Bank, where Rhodes had a checking account. She had bright red hair, though Ivy had assured Rhodes that particular shade of red was rarely seen in either the plant or animal world except on Lorene. It was the color of embarrassed orange. Lorene had been married three times, two of them to the same man.

"But I wasn't in there with her," Lorene went on. "I was over in the main building with Claudia and Jan."

A woman with short blond hair and blue eyes nodded. Standing next to her was a short, scholarly-looking woman with black hair. She nodded, too.

"So you can see that I didn't kill her," Lorene said. "And I have no idea who did."

"Who was in the room across the hall?" Rhodes asked, but it turned out that no one had been in that room, either. The closest occupied room had been the one shared by Vernell and Carrie.

"What did you hear before the screaming?" Rhodes asked.

"Yelling," Carrie said. "It was more like yelling."

"Right. And before the yelling, what did you hear?"

"That's the funny part," Carrie said. "I didn't hear a thing."

"How about you, Vernell?"

"Not a thing," Vernell said quickly, a little too quickly to suit Rhodes.

"You're sure about that?"

"I'm sure," Vernell said.

While he was talking and asking questions, Rhodes moved around the room, trying to see if anyone's shoes or robe or pants were damp, but he really couldn't tell. Besides, any dampness would most likely have had time to dry before he arrived. Of course the bottoms of Chatterton's pants were wet, and so were his shoes, but Chatterton had been standing outside when Rhodes arrived, and then he'd walked around the building with Rhodes to show him Henrietta's room.

Rhodes continued asking questions, and it was beginning to appear that everyone had an alibi, or claimed to. Everyone had been talking to someone else, or within sight of someone else, when Henrietta had begun to yell. That was the appearance, at least. Rhodes wasn't sure how closely it matched the reality. With that many people milling around, it was possible for someone to have slipped away unnoticed and then returned.

And while everyone seemed appalled at Henrietta's death, two of the women were talking quietly together about motive, means, and opportunity. They seemed to know quite a bit about police work.

Rhodes paid special attention to them. It turned out that they were two of the writers, Marian Willoughby and Belinda Marshall, both of whom told Rhodes that they were hoping to write mystery novels.

"Janet Evanovich broke out of the romance ghetto with mystery novels," Marian said. "That's why it's so exciting to be involved with a real murder. It might be material for a book."

Marian was short, with brown hair and brown eyes, and a determined chin. She was the only one there wearing jeans. She looked like a normal person, but Rhodes knew better. He was pretty sure no normal person would look at someone's death as material for a book.

"In the first place, we don't know that there's been a murder," Rhodes said. "It might have been just an accident."

"Maybe," Belinda Marshall said. She was a tall woman with an elongated face and very long hair that hung down her back in a heavy braid. "But maybe not. A writer has to be alert to all kinds of things. Maybe we can even help you find out who did it."

All Rhodes needed was a dormitory full of people trying to help him solve a murder.

"I'll have plenty of professional help," he said. "Were both of you in the main building when the problem developed?"

"Is that what you call it?" Marian asked. "A problem?"

Rhodes almost expected her to start taking notes.

"It's not a technical term," he said.

Marian considered his question. "I was in the other building so I didn't hear anything," she said. "I don't know about Belinda."

Belinda looked surprised. She said, "Yes you do. I'd just been talking to you when someone ran over to tell us that there'd been a murder."

Marian shrugged. "If you say so."

Belinda looked as if she'd like to take Marian aside and shake her. Rhodes thought she might have done it, but they were interrupted just then by the arrival of the ambulance and Ruth Grady, who had hardly stepped inside the dormitory when someone else showed up, someone about whom Rhodes had nearly forgotten.

Terry Don Coslin followed Ruth into the sitting room and looked around. He was wearing a T-shirt that hugged his iron-hard pecs and stomach, and his jeans were so tight Rhodes wondered how he could breathe.

Terry Don yawned and looked around the room as if he had no clue that anything out of the ordinary had happened and said, "What's all the excitement about?"

According to Terry Don, he'd left the main building after dinner, gone back to his room in the president's house, and read a few chapters from a book he'd brought with him, and gone to sleep.

Rhodes could tell by the looks on the writers' faces that each one of them hoped it had been her book he was reading, which was no doubt why Terry Don had carefully avoided mentioning a title. Ruth Grady didn't look as if she cared whether he'd been reading or not; she was just starstruck.

Rhodes told her to wait outside for the justice of the peace and then take him in to have a look at Henrietta.

"Her room's at the end of the hall," Rhodes said. "As soon as the JP pronounces her dead, you do the crime scene."

"All right. Any chance that Terry Don Coslin needs a body search? I volunteer."

"I'll let you know," Rhodes said.

There were still a few things that worried him about the stories that he'd heard, and he also had a few questions for Terry Don, but all that could wait. He wasn't having much luck with the whole group around, so he wanted to talk to people individually. Besides, he had another stop to make. He told everyone that they could go to their rooms.

"Except for you, Lorene," he said. "You'll have to find somewhere else."

"There's another room in the president's house," Chatterton said. "She can stay there."

There were several envious looks in Lorene's direction until Rhodes told her that she couldn't get anything from the room where Henrietta was.

"It's a crime scene now," he explained.

"What if it was just an accident?" Marian Willoughby asked sarcastically.

"Then it won't be a crime scene anymore. But until we find out for sure, no one can go in there. You'll just have to do the best you can, Lorene."

"Oh, pooh. I'll just go home to Clearview and sleep in my own bed tonight. I couldn't sleep in this place anyhow, not after what happened to Henrietta. I'll get some things together before tomorrow evening, though. I don't want to miss any of the conference."

"That's fine," Rhodes said. "That is, it's fine if Mr. Chatterton can find you another room. We'll have the other one sealed off for a while."

"I hope you don't think I wanted to stay in *there*," Lorene said.

Rhodes said he hadn't thought she'd want to.

"Now then," he said, "let's break it up here and see if you can all get some sleep."

It was nearly one o'clock by that time, and Rhodes wouldn't have minded getting some sleep himself. But he didn't have time for sleeping.

Thomas Chatterton followed him out of the dormitory.

"Do you think it will be all right for us to continue the conference?" he asked when they were outside.

"I don't see why not," Rhodes said. "I'll be back out tomorrow, and I'll have to talk to some people, but I'll try not to disrupt things too much."

Chatterton didn't appear convinced, and Rhodes didn't blame him for being skeptical. It wasn't easy to have a murder investigation without disrupting things. And he was certain it was murder. People didn't yell when there was no one around, and Rhodes was sure someone had been in the room when Henrietta had died.

"This isn't the way I thought things would be," Chatterton said.

"Nobody ever thinks they'll have trouble like this," Rhodes told him.

"Yes, but it's just so horrible. Especially if that woman was murdered. It means that the killer is right here, taking part in the conference. Doesn't it?"

"Probably," Rhodes said.

"Good Lord," Chatterton said.

Rhodes couldn't think of any response to that, so he got in the county car and drove away.

6

▼

THE APPLEBY PLACE WAS ON A DIRT ROAD JUST DOWN THE HILL from the college. Rhodes had been there before, and he didn't have any trouble finding it.

Even in the dark, the place looked better than it had when Cy Appleby had been around. Then the yard had been mostly churned-up mud that got hard as rock when it hadn't rained for a while, but now there were patches of grass growing on it. The drooping roof had been reshingled, and the windows all had fairly new screens. The two hackberry trees in the yard didn't look any healthier than they ever had, but then you couldn't expect too much from hackberry trees.

There was a light on in the front room, so Rhodes went up on the porch and knocked. One of the twins, either Claude or Clyde, opened the door.

"Hey, Sheriff," he said.

He was a big, moon-faced young man with blue eyes and cottony hair, and he looked exactly like his twin brother, so exactly, in fact, that Rhodes couldn't tell them apart.

"I guess you're here about the naked woman," Clyde said. Or Claude.

"Your mother made the call," Rhodes said.

"That's right. She's here. Come on in."

Rhodes went inside and saw that the interior of the house had also been improved. There was a new RCA TV set, a new couch, and a new rug on the old wood floor. The rocking chair in which Mrs. Appleby sat was the oldest thing in the room. The other twin, Claude, or possibly Clyde, was lounging on the couch, with one leg drooping over the arm. He and his mother were watching an ancient episode of *Mama's Family,* which he muted with the remote.

"Hey, Sheriff," Clyde said.

Or maybe it was Claude. Rhodes decided to ask and was surprised to discover that he'd been right with his first guess.

"I'm the good-looking one, if that helps you any," Clyde said.

Rhodes said he appreciated the tip.

"And how have you been doing, Mrs. Appleby?" he asked.

"Tolerable," she said.

Rhodes thought she looked better than that, without Cy there to beat her up.

"Where's Twyla Faye keeping herself?" he asked.

"She's in Waco, going to beauty school," Clyde said. "Says she's gonna make thirty thousand dollars a year, just cuttin' hair. You believe that, Sheriff?"

Rhodes said he wasn't sure how much money a person could make by cutting hair.

"Says the tips are real good if you got a good clientele," Clyde went on. "That's the word she used. *Clientele.* I don't think she's planning on coming back to Obert to work. There's not a whole lot of clientele here."

"What about you boys?" Rhodes asked. "Still working at Wal-Mart?"

"Yes, sir," Clyde said.

"And doin' real well, too," his mother said. "The both of them. Clyde's going to be the manager of the automotive center, and Claude's been put in charge of sporting goods."

Rhodes said that he was glad to hear it. He'd gotten them the jobs they'd started out in, and he was pleased that they'd made the most of their chance. He'd been afraid they might turn out like their father.

"I guess you didn't come here to talk about my family, though," Mrs. Appleby said.

"No," Rhodes admitted. "I came about your phone call."

"The naked woman," Claude said, grinning broadly.

"That's right. Who saw her?"

"Well, it wasn't me," Claude said.

"Me, neither," Clyde said. "I wish it had been, though."

"You hush your mouth, Clyde Appleby," his mother said. "You should be ashamed of yourself."

Clyde grinned at Claude, who grinned back. As far as Rhodes could tell, neither one of them was the least bit ashamed.

"What time did you see this woman?" Rhodes asked Mrs. Applebly.

"It wasn't long after David Letterman was over," she said, turning her attention back to him. "Claude and Clyde like to watch that Top Ten list of his, and he's got to where sometimes he doesn't give it out until the show's practically over. That's the way it was tonight, which is why I was up so late."

Rhodes knew that Mrs. Appleby hadn't seen the naked woman on Letterman's show, though he supposed it was possible that she had. Rhodes seemed to remember something about an incident with Drew Barrymore.

"Ma went outside to get some air," Claude said. "She does that every night before she goes to bed unless the weather's bad. That's when she saw that woman."

"Makes me wish I'd gone for some air, myself," Clyde said.

"You hush," Mrs. Appleby said. "You know better than to talk like that."

"Shoot," Clyde said. "You should hear how they talk down at the Wal-Mart. And I mean the customers, not just the people who work there."

"Never mind," Rhodes said. This was getting as bad as trying to get information from Hack and Lawton. "Can you show me where you saw her, Mrs. Appleby?"

"Come on outside and I can," she said, getting out of the rocker.

Rhodes followed her out through the kitchen. She pushed open a door, and went down some concrete steps into the back yard. Rhodes stood beside her, and she pointed toward the back of the yard where several tall trees grew. Over the tops of the trees, Rhodes could see the main building of the college on top of the hill, looking even more like a castle from a Universal horror movie than ever.

"I was standing right here," Mrs. Appleby said. "And she was right back there."

The moon was going down, and it was quite dark back in the trees, which were about fifty yards away. Rhodes wondered how well Mrs. Appleby could have seen anyone.

"Are you sure it was a woman?" Rhodes asked.

Mrs. Appleby half turned her head to look at him.

"There's ways to tell, Sheriff," she said.

"Right," Rhodes said. "But the light's not good, and—"

"It was better then. The moon was up more, and I could see all right. It's against the law to run naked right out in the open, isn't it?"

Rhodes said that public nudity was a misdemeanor in the state of Texas.

"That is, it's a misdemeanor if anyone was offended by it."

"Well, I was sure enough offended," Mrs. Appleby said. "And

I'm just glad that Claude and Clyde didn't see it. They may joke about it, but it's not right for boys their age to see things like that."

Rhodes didn't want to speculate on what it was right for Claude and Clyde to see. Thanks to a previous investigation, he knew for a fact that the twins' choice in magazines had exposed them to a certain amount of female nudity long before now.

"Did you see where she came from?" he asked.

"Not exactly," Mrs. Appleby said. "I think she saw me before I saw her. She was headed into the trees when I saw her, so I guess that's where she came from. She saw me, and she turned and ran."

Rhodes thought about it. It wasn't far from the college to where they were standing, not if someone had come straight down the hill. There wasn't really anything in between except the trees. A naked woman could have come from just about anywhere, he supposed, but considering that there was a big concentration of women on the college campus, and considering that they were unfamiliar with the area and might easily get lost, it seemed pretty likely that the woman was someone from the writers' conference.

That possibility raised more questions than it answered, how-ever. What was she doing naked in the first place? And why was she running around in the woods? And did any of that have something to do with Henrietta Bayam's death?

Because of the time element, Rhodes was sure the two events were connected. He didn't much believe in coincidence, even though Ivy liked to tell him that life was full of outrageous co-incidences, and he'd seen some himself.

"She didn't say anything?" Rhodes asked.

"Just ran."

"And you didn't see her face?"

"No. She was going the wrong way for that."

Rhodes hated to ask the next question, but he did it anyway.

"And you're sure she was naked?"

"She was wearing a pair of those bikini underpants," Mrs. Appleby said. "But that doesn't count. Does it?"

Rhodes wasn't sure whether someone wearing bikini underpants could be accused of public nudity or not. It was clearly a case for a brilliant lawyer, assuming the woman ever turned up and assuming that Mrs. Appleby still wanted to press charges.

"What color?" he asked.

"Red, I think."

Rhodes thought Mrs. Appleby must have much better eyesight than he did. On the other hand, if a naked woman were running through his back yard, his eyesight might improve.

"Did you notice anything else about her? Height? Hair color?"

Mrs. Appleby shook her head. "No. She was gone real quick."

"Why don't you go back inside," Rhodes said. "I want to look around back there."

"You got a flashlight?"

Rhodes started to say that he had one in the county car, but Mrs. Appleby didn't give him the chance.

"Because I could send Claude out with one if that'd help you," she told him.

"Why don't you do that," Rhodes said.

He had a few questions for Claude, anyway. When the boy came outside with the flashlight, Rhodes said, "Now tell me about the naked woman, Claude."

Claude gave Rhodes the flashlight and tried to look innocent. It didn't work.

"I don't know what you mean, Sheriff," he said.

That didn't work, either.

"Yes you do," Rhodes said. "I saw you grinning at Clyde in there. You saw something. Maybe both of you did."

Claude shook his head. "Dang it, Sheriff, I never can put anything over on you, can I?"

"Sure you can. You've done it before, and you might even do

it again. But not this time. Now tell me what you saw."

"Well, I guess I will. But you have to promise you won't tell Ma."

Rhodes said he wouldn't tell.

"Okay. When she went out back, I decided to go out with her. I don't usually, but it was a nice night, and I thought, why not. I could sort of keep her company. I think she gets lonesome sometimes with Twyla Faye gone and Daddy in the pen."

Rhodes believed him, though he had a hard time figuring out why anyone would miss a man like Cy Appleby. Ivy had tried to explain it to him, and he knew it was possible. He just had trouble with it.

"Anyway," Claude said, "I was about to go out the back door when I saw that woman. I didn't see much, though. She was already heading back into the trees."

"But she was naked, right?"

"If you can call it that. I think she had on a little pair of panties. Tell you the truth, I couldn't see that much. I was look-ing through the screen door, after all."

"So you wouldn't recognize the woman if you saw her again."

"Not a chance. Not even if you just showed me her back."

"All right," Rhodes said. "You can go on back in. I'll bring the flashlight to the door when I'm finished with it."

Claude nodded and turned back toward the house.

Rhodes headed for the trees. He could hear a dog barking persistently off to the left. Must be a stray cat, Rhodes thought, shining the light on the ground in front of him and swinging it from side to side, looking for anything that resembled a clue.

He didn't see a single thing, but he kept on going, thinking that he might have been better off to wait until morning and come back in the daylight. In the dark, he was about as likely to mess things up as he was to find anything of significance, assuming that there was anything to find.

But he kept going. He was almost to the trees when the shoot-ing started.

7

▼

RHODES STOPPED AND LISTENED. THE SHOTS SOUNDED AS IF they'd come from somewhere nearby, probably from a shotgun. Rhodes started running in what he hoped was the right direction.

When he got into the trees, he had to be careful. Running through a woods in the dark could be hazardous to a person's physical well-being, even if the person was carrying a flashlight, mainly because it was impossible to shine the light on the ground to see what was in front of you and to shine it on the tree limbs that reached out to grab you from all sides at the same time.

Rhodes elected to shine the light on the ground, which turned out to be a mistake. A limb that he didn't see caught him just under the eye, popped his head backward, and brought him to a sudden stop.

"Hold it right there, you sorry window-peeping son of a bitch," a man yelled, though not at Rhodes, who was standing in the dark woods rubbing his eye and wondering what had happened to the flashlight.

"If you even look like you're gonna move, I'll fill you full of number twelve buckshot," the man yelled.

Rhodes looked down at his feet. The flashlight was there, sending a strong yellow beam through the wet leaves. Rhodes picked it up and shined it off to his left. He didn't see any more treacherous-looking limbs, so he started walking toward where he'd heard the voice. The barking that Rhodes had heard earlier was louder.

A shotgun blasted. Rhodes ducked instinctively, though the shot passed well over him. Leaves and sticks pattered down on his head.

"Who's that comin' through there?" the voice yelled. "You better stop right where you are. That shot was just a warnin'. Don't think I'm scared of two of you! I got three more shells in this here gun, and I'm loaded for bear!"

"Just hold your fire," Rhodes said. "I'm the sheriff."

"Yeah, I'll bet that's right. You're the sheriff, and I'm the Lone Ranger. You just stay right where you are. I've got your friend here in my sights, and if you show up yourself, I'll let him have it."

"Do that, and you'll be spending your time in the county jail while you wait for a free ride to prison," Rhodes said. "I'm fixing to come out of the trees, so you just hold your fire."

"Be damned if I do. There's not gonna be any more window-peeping around here. Just gonna be two dead window-peepers."

"I don't think so," said a voice from the darkness behind the man with the shotgun.

Rhodes recognized the voice. Ruth Grady had arrived on the scene.

"Just lay the shotgun on the ground, sir," Ruth said.

"Damn," the voice said. "You know how to use that pistol, little lady?"

"Yes, sir, I do," Ruth said. "Now lay the shotgun down and back away from it. Slowly."

"Damn. I guess that really is the sheriff out there in those trees, then, and not some window-peeper. Am I right?"

"That you, Sheriff?" Ruth called.

"It's me," Rhodes said. He rubbed his eye. "What's left of me."

"Damn," the voice said. "All right. I'm puttin' it down. But don't you let that window-peeper get away."

"Don't you worry about that, sir," Ruth said. "I'll take good care of him."

Rhodes walked out of the trees and shined the flashlight on the scene. There was a house not too far away, and in its big back yard Ruth Grady stood, holding her pistol in a two-handed grip and pointing at a skinny man wearing overalls and no shirt. He was somewhere in his sixties, Rhodes guessed, and he was backing away from the shotgun which he'd laid at his feet as Ruth had told him to do.

And not too far from where Rhodes emerged from the trees was Terry Don Coslin, who looked as if he wished he'd never agreed to pay a visit to his old home county.

Terry Don didn't sound sorry to be back in Blacklin County. He looked up at the dark sky and said, "You live in a city long enough, you forget how many stars there are up there."

"You should come back more often," Rhodes said.

Terry Don brought his gaze back to earth and turned to look at Rhodes.

"Maybe so. Didn't I sign a book for you at the Wal-Mart this afternoon?"

"You did," Rhodes said. "But we're a long way from there now."

"You damn sure are," said the man in the overalls. "You're on my property, is where you are, and I'd be within my rights if I shot the whole damn lot of you."

"I don't know about that," Rhodes told him. "A law officer in pursuit of his duty"—he looked at Ruth "—or *her* duty can enter your property legally. It's not like you have any fences up, except that one over there around your dog pen. You think you could get that dog to stop barking?"

"Keep it down, Grover!" the man yelled, and the dog stopped barking.

"Thanks," Rhodes said, who really did appreciate it. His head was throbbing from being hit by the tree limb.

"You're not welcome. And I'll tell you something else. I'm damn well gonna build me a good strong fence around this whole place. It's been like a damn parade through here tonight. People tramping all over the damn place, and peepin' in my window besides. If you're really the sheriff, and I guess you are, you might as well arrest that son of a bitch over there and take him away."

"And the complaint would be?"

"Window-peepin'," the man said. "Haven't you been listenin' to a damn word I've said?"

"I've been listening. Now I'm going to pick up your shotgun, Mr.—" Rhodes stopped, then continued. "I don't think you've introduced yourself."

"Billy Quentin is my name. And this is my property you're on. You say it's legal for you to be here, and maybe it is, for you. But it's not for that damn window-peeper."

Rhodes picked up the shotgun, and Ruth Grady relaxed her stance.

"I think you can put the sidearm away," Rhodes told her. "Mr. Quentin isn't going to hurt anybody."

"Not unless it's a window-peeper," Quentin said.

"I think he means you," Rhodes said to Coslin. "What are you doing out here?"

"I wasn't window-peeping," Terry Don said. "I was just taking a walk. I went back to the president's house, but Chatterton was fussing around and talking so much that I knew I wasn't going to get any sleep. Besides, I was upset about what had happened to Henrietta. So I thought I'd go outside and walk around, get a look at all those stars up there. I was going to stay pretty much on the college campus, but I must've gotten lost."

"Damn right you did," Quentin said. "You're on my property now. Damn window-peeper."

"I wasn't peeping in any windows," Terry Don said evenly. "I didn't even get close to your house."

"Bullcorn. You're the one that came by peepin' on me a couple of hours ago, and you're the one I caught out here this time. Don't tell me you're not a window-peeper."

Terry Don didn't look like a window-peeper to Rhodes, but then he'd known killers who looked like they might just have been elected president of a Sunday school class.

"You say someone was out here earlier?" Rhodes said to Quentin.

"Damn right there was. And that's him."

"How do you know? Did you see him up close?"

Quentin passed a hand under an overall strap and scratched his armpit.

"Well," he said, "not exactly."

"How exactly?" Rhodes asked.

Quentin hemmed and hawed and finally said, "There was damn sure somebody on my property. Grover was barkin' his head off. But whoever it was, he was gone before I got out here with my shotgun."

"So you didn't actually see anybody."

"What difference does that make?"

"Because it might even have been a woman who was running around down here earlier, not a man. Are you sure you didn't see anybody?"

"It wasn't any woman," Quentin said. "It was that window-peeper. I caught up with him this time, and there he is. You oughta arrest him instead of standin' around here wastin' my time."

Rhodes wasn't going to arrest anyone, not just yet, not until he'd figured out what was going on. He told Terry Don to get on up the hill.

"I'll be talking to you tomorrow," he said. "I hope you'll be sticking around the conference."

"That's what I'm getting paid for," Terry Don said.

"All right, then. You can go on back up there."

Terry Don turned and started back up the hill.

"You can't just let him go like that," Quentin protested.

"Yes I can," Rhodes said. "I'm the sheriff."

"Till the next election, you are. Then I'll by God vote you out."

Rhodes wished he had a dime for every time he'd heard that one, or a variation of it. But he didn't say so. Instead he commended Quentin for his willingness to take part in the democratic process.

"Bullcorn," Quentin said.

"That's what some people think," Rhodes conceded. "But I'm not one of them."

Then he ejected the shells from the shotgun and handed it to Quentin.

"You're gonna be sorry about this mess, Sheriff," Quentin said.

"I probably will," Rhodes said. "Are you through with that crime scene, Deputy Grady?"

"Not yet," Ruth said. "But when I heard shooting, I thought I'd better get down here and check it out. Looks like it was a good thing I came."

"Lucky for that damn window-peeper," Quentin said.

"Lucky for you, too," Rhodes told him. To Ruth he said, "I'll meet you up there at the college in a little while. Right now I have to return a flashlight."

They left Quentin standing there with his shotgun. Rhodes hadn't gone far before Grover started barking again.

Rhodes heard Quentin say, "Oh, shut up, Grover," and smiled in spite of himself.

8

▼

"I'D GUESS SHE FELL AND HIT HER HEAD ON THE CORNER OF the dresser," Ruth Grady said.

She and Rhodes were standing in the room where Henrietta had died. The body had been removed, but there was still a stain on the floor where Henrietta's head had lain.

The dormitory was quiet. Rhodes wondered just how many of the writers were asleep. Henrietta's death must have disturbed a few of them, though they hadn't really shown it.

"You think it was an accident, then?" Rhodes said.

"Not hardly. See that window screen over there?"

Rhodes nodded. He'd noticed it earlier.

"Somebody pushed it open and went out that way," Ruth said. "There are signs on the outside, too."

"Footprints?"

"We're not that lucky. The grass is mashed down. That's about all." Ruth looked around the room. "Did you know she was naked under that robe?"

"I didn't check," Rhodes said. "Does it mean anything?"

"Maybe not. Maybe she was just getting ready for bed. But

what if she and the somebody who went out that window were getting ready to make a little whoopie?"

"Terry Don?" Rhodes said.

"Or Chatterton."

"He says he was working out in the parlor, getting things in order."

"He says."

"Right. I'll make sure."

"And there's another possibility, too," Ruth said.

"There is?"

"You don't have to play innocent with me, Sheriff. You know as well as I do that there might have been another woman in here."

"I don't know about that. There would've been gossip about Henrietta if that were the case."

"You don't hear everything," Ruth said.

"True. What about you?"

"I hadn't heard anything about that. But it's still a possibility."

"I didn't know about Henrietta's feud with Vernell, either," Rhodes said. "What about you?"

"I heard that story," Ruth said. "And that brings up a question. Where was Vernell when this happened?"

"In her room."

"She says."

"So does Carrie Logan," Rhodes said. "Her roomie."

"Oh. Well, maybe Vernell didn't do it, then. But I wouldn't rule her out."

"I won't. What do you think happened here?"

Ruth took some Polaroid pictures from her shirt pocket.

"Look," she said, handing one of them to Rhodes. "See the way she was lying?"

Rhodes took the photo and looked at it. It showed him what he'd already seen previously when he'd looked into the room with Chatterton.

"There's a little blood under her head there," he said. "The stain's still on the floor."

"I think she fell and hit her head on the corner of the dresser," Ruth said. "And that's what killed her. I guess Dr. White will let us know for sure."

"I thought you said it wasn't an accident."

"That's right. Someone was with her, and I think there was a struggle. See how the bed's messed up?"

"Well, you said she was making whoopie," Rhodes pointed out.

"That would mess up the covers, all right, but not exactly like they are now."

Rhodes was tempted to ask Ruth how she knew, but he didn't want her to think he was prying into her sex life. Besides, he thought she was right.

"You think someone came in and surprised her on the bed with someone else?"

"No. Someone might have come in, but it wasn't a surprise. I'm sure Henrietta would have locked the door. And if she didn't, whoever was in here with her would have."

Rhodes thought that was right, too. He certainly would have locked the door if he'd been in that room with Henrietta.

"What about fingerprints?" Rhodes asked.

"I'll check for them before I leave," Ruth said. "But do you think they'll really do us any good?"

"Maybe. Maybe not."

Rhodes thought the "not" was more likely. Even if there were prints, they probably wouldn't be on file anywhere. And he didn't think it was going to be easy getting everyone at the conference to volunteer to be printed. If it came down to it, however, he'd just have to coerce them.

"Anything else you can tell by looking around?"

"You can see the way the throw rug's messed up," Ruth said.

"Another sign of a struggle. But that's about it. If we're lucky, Dr. White can tell us more."

Rhodes knew it was going to take more than luck. It always did. He was convinced that someone attending the conference had been lying to him from the beginning because he didn't think Henrietta had been killed by some outsider just passing by. The trick would be to find out who the liar was.

Rhodes was sure it wouldn't be easy. After all, he was dealing with a group of women who were liars by profession, or who wanted to be. That was undoubtedly going to complicate things.

And then there was that naked woman the Applebys had seen running around. Rhodes figured that the woman had been the one who had disturbed Quentin the first time. Too bad he hadn't gotten a look at her.

"I'm going home," Rhodes told Ruth. "Tomorrow I'll be back early to search those woods down there. I got interrupted tonight."

"You never told me what you were doing there in the first place," Ruth said.

Rhodes told her about the naked woman.

"And you think she had something to do with Henrietta?"

"Don't you?"

"Maybe it was just some city woman who wanted to get close to nature."

"Nobody wants to get that close to nature, not at this time of the year," Rhodes said.

"What if she's the one who was in the room with Henrietta?"

"I guess that's something we'll have to consider."

"You think she dropped her glass slipper in Billy Quentin's back yard?"

Rhodes smiled. "It would be a big help if she did."

"Yeah. Well, I wouldn't count on it if I were you."

"I try never to count on anything when it comes to a crime like this one," Rhodes said. "That way I'm never disappointed."

"You'd be disappointed if Clyde and Claude were involved in this, wouldn't you?"

Rhodes had to admit that he would. He'd tried to help the twins, and it seemed that they had their lives on the right track. He didn't like to think that they could have had anything to do with Henrietta's death.

"You don't think that's possible, do you?" he said.

"I wouldn't rule them out. When it comes to sneaking around and peeping in windows, those two have a head start on everybody else around here."

"They've changed," Rhodes said. "At least I think they've changed."

Ruth looked skeptical. She said, "Anything's possible, I guess."

But she didn't sound as if she meant a word of it.

Rhodes wasn't what he could call perky the next morning. He'd had only a couple of hours' sleep, and his eyes felt as if they were glued shut with rubber cement. It was one of those times that Rhodes wished he liked coffee. He had a Dr Pepper instead, but the caffeine didn't kick in enough to make any difference.

Hack woke him up, however. When Rhodes walked through the door of the jail, Hack said, "You better go talk to Mildred Cramer. She got one of those calls about the contest."

"What contest?" Rhodes asked.

"That one about the date with Terry Don."

"Oh," Rhodes said, rubbing his eyes, one of which was still sore from where the tree limb had whacked him.

"What about it?" he asked.

"She says she knows who did the calling," Hack told him.

Rhodes stopped rubbing.

"Who was it?"

"Henrietta Bayam," Hack said.

9

▼

MILDRED CRAMER AND HER HUSBAND, JOE, LIVED IN A LITTLE white frame house just outside the city limits on the road to Milsby. They had chickens in a pen and a collie dog named Hank that Rhodes wished wasn't quite so friendly.

"Get down, Hank," Mildred called from her front porch. "Don't you jump up on the sheriff like that. He doesn't want your paw prints all over his shirt."

Hank paid her no attention at all. He kept trying to jump up on Rhodes until he saw a cat zip past the corner of the house. He left Rhodes in the lurch and went charging off after the cat, who was headed for a little sheet-metal barn out back.

"Don't worry about Princess," Mildred said, meaning the cat, Rhodes supposed. "She can take care of herself. Sometimes I think Hank must not be too smart. He's never caught her yet, but he keeps on trying."

Mildred was around sixty. She was short and stout, and she was sitting on her small front porch in a lawn chair with her left leg stuck straight out in front of her. Her left foot was in a cast that rested on an overturned bucket.

"It's not as uncomfortable as it looks," she said. "Sometimes it itches under the cast, though. That's not much fun."

"What happened?" Rhodes asked.

"I stepped in a hole on the way to the barn, broke my ankle. Teach me to look where I'm going, I guess."

There was a TV tray beside Mildred. On the tray were a portable telephone, a battery-powered radio, and a glass of something that Rhodes guessed was water. Mildred turned down the radio, which had been tuned in to a talk show from Dallas, and reached for the glass.

"Lemonade," she said, taking a drink and setting the glass back on the table. "Joe made it for me before he went to work. I'd offer you some, but the one glass is all I have. It's instant, though, and you can make one for yourself if you want to. The stuff's in the kitchen."

Rhodes didn't want to. He liked lemonade just fine, in the summertime, but it wasn't summer, and he wasn't thirsty.

"No, thanks," he said. "You called about Henrietta Bayam."

"Poor thing. I heard about her this morning from Annie Floyd I couldn't believe it, and I'd just talked to her yesterday."

"About some radio contest?"

"That's right. A date with Terry Don Coslin." Mildred laughed. "Be my luck, I'd win. With this foot, I couldn't go anyway. I can walk on it, but it's not easy, and I have to use a cane."

Rhodes saw that there was a wooden cane hooked to the arm of the lawn chair.

"About that phone call," he said.

"I knew it was a joke right off," Mildred said. "Imagine Henrietta trying to fool me like that."

"She called several other people," Rhodes said. "And none of them recognized her voice."

"Well, I did. I've been in her writing group for so long that

I've heard her read all kinds of things. I'd know that voice any-where."

Rhodes heard barking back in the barn and looked in that direction.

"Princess is probably up on a couple of hay bales where Hank can't get at her," Mildred said. "Like I said, you don't have to worry about her."

"I was worried about Hank," Rhodes said.

Mildred laughed. "He'll be all right. When he gets himself all barked out, he'll come and lie down in the shade till he recovers."

"So you're sure it was Henrietta who called," Rhodes said, getting back to the purpose of his visit.

"I'm sure, all right. As soon as I caught on, I said, 'Henrietta, you ought to know better than to try to fool an old woman like me.' "

"Did she say why she was doing it?"

"No. She just hung up. But it was her, all right. I remember when she was reading from *Love's Wild Deception,* she used a voice like that."

"That's a book?" Rhodes asked.

"Yes. One of her better ones, too, even if it hasn't ever been published. Or maybe it has. Some people think Vernell stole the plot from it for her own book."

"What do you think?"

Mildred took another drink of lemonade, set the glass back down, and leaned slightly forward in her chair.

"Do you read romance novels, Sheriff?"

"I read Vernell's."

"Is that the only one?"

Rhodes admitted that it was.

"Well, then you don't know. But the truth is that they're a lot alike. I don't mean there's a formula or anything like that. But I'm working on one myself, and it's a whole lot the same. In quite a few romance novels, you have the same situation. There's a woman who's got some kind of problem, and she meets this man that really irritates her, or seems to. The readers all know that the two of them were meant to be together, but things keep getting in the way. There's usually another man, and we all know he's definitely the wrong one, but it looks like he's going to get her by fair means or foul, and the troubles just keep piling up. I'd say that Vernell's book is like that. So was Henrietta's. But then so are a few hundred more."

Rhodes asked why Mildred wasn't at the conference. She pointed to her foot.

"If it weren't for that ankle, I'd be right there. I'd love to meet that Jeanne Arnot. She's sold more books than anybody in New York."

Rhodes said he was sorry about the ankle and about Mildred's having to miss the conference. Mildred didn't seem the type to write romance novels, but apparently there wasn't a type. He should have known that.

Rhodes had another stop to make before he went out and visited Billy Quentin's woods. He wanted to have a look at Henrietta Bayam's house. She had lived only about six blocks from downtown Clearview, and Rhodes drove through town to get there.

He noticed that the rubble from some recently-collapsed buildings had been cleared away sometime within the last few days, but the sight of the vacant lot on what had been one of the busiest corners in the town didn't do much to cheer him up about Clearview's prospects for the future.

He turned left at the corner and drove past two more blocks of what had once been called "the business district." There wasn't much business being conducted there now. There was still a fairly prosperous bank on one corner, but most of the rest of the buildings in the block were vacant.

On the other side of the street there was one store, a vacant building, and a parking lot. The building where one of the town's biggest grocery stores had once been was empty now, the store having moved into larger quarters out on the highway near the Wal-Mart. Rhodes figured that in another year or two there wouldn't be a business left in the business district, with the possible exception of the bank. He wondered if anyone would come up with a new name for it then.

Henrietta had lived in an old brick house with a neatly trimmed yard. The house had belonged to her parents, who had died about ten years previously when Henrietta was barely out of high school, her father in a car accident and her mother of cancer. As far as Rhodes knew, she didn't have any other relatives. She was the last of the Bayams. She'd been married once, just after her graduation from college, but the marriage hadn't lasted very long. Rhodes didn't know why. After that, she had moved back to Clearview and started working as a secretary to the town's only optometrist. She'd been there ever since.

Rhodes pulled the county car into the driveway and got out. He stood for a minute and looked the place over. There was a walled concrete porch on the front, with short brick pillars on either side of the steps. The windows were all covered with screens painted black, and there was a black screen door in front.

Rhodes went up on the porch, opened the screen, and tried the front door. It wasn't locked. Most people in Clearview still trusted their neighbors and didn't bother to lock either their houses or their cars, though more and more of them were beginning to do so.

Rhodes went inside. The front room was chilly. It smelled musty and looked like something out of a nineteenth-century novel. There were a couple of old chairs and an overstuffed couch with lace doilies on the arms. To the right was another room that connected to the living room by what Rhodes thought were called French doors for some reason he'd forgotten, if he'd ever known.

Henrietta had been using the room as an office. Bookshelves overflowed with paperback romance novels, fat ones, thin ones, and medium-sized ones. A computer desk stood against one wall and held a monitor, keyboard, and printer. The computer box was on the floor underneath. It seemed that every house Rhodes looked into in the course of an investigation had a computer these days, convincing proof to Rhodes that the computer revolution had touched everyone in the world.

Rhodes opened the French doors and went into the room. There was a cardboard box beside the printer, and Rhodes opened it up to have a look. What he saw was the title page of a manuscript. Rhodes picked it up to read it, then put it back down. If he left it in the box, he could just about read it without having to put on his glasses.

The title page said:

A ROMANTIC WAY TO DIE
A Mystery Novel

BY
Henrietta Bayam

Ivy must have been right, Rhodes thought. Everyone who wasn't writing a romance novel was writing a mystery, and Henrietta was writing both.

He got his reading glasses out of his pocket and took out a few pages of the manuscript to read. The very first sentence grabbed his attention.

Bernell Kidsey was a bitch, it said.

Uh-oh, Rhodes thought. Then he read the next two sentences: *She was also a thief. That's why I had to kill her.*

Rhodes forgot about going to the woods to look for clues. He took the manuscript into the other room, turned on a light, and sat on the couch, which was a lot more comfortable than it looked.

Then he started to read.

10

▼

AFTER READING AS FAST AS HE COULD FOR A COUPLE OF HOURS, Rhodes put the manuscript aside. It had become clear to him after only a few pages that the book was based mostly on people in and around Clearview, and a few from out of town, with the character of Bernell Kidsey being only the first of many examples.

The plot was simple: an aspiring romance novelist writes a book that all her friends tell her is a cinch to be published just as soon as the manuscript is polished and ready, but an envious friend steals the plot idea and pitches a much inferior version of the book to a sleazy agent named "Jane Arnold," who isn't above sleeping with editors (either men or women; Jane wasn't particular) to increase her sales records.

The book's narrator, the practically saintly (except for her murderous tendencies) was "Loretta Seaham," and she managed to kill the treacherous Bernell and get the crime blamed on Arnold, who conveniently committed suicide, thus convincing the slightly stupid redneck county sheriff ("Don Street") of her guilt and allowing Loretta to get on with her life and her interrupted writing career with no one the wiser.

Rhodes folded his glasses and put them back in his pocket. His only consolation was that Henrietta had made him somewhat younger, trimmer, and better-looking than he actually was. Well, younger anyway. Ivy had been keeping him pretty much on a healthy diet since their marriage, and he'd shed a few pounds. Maybe he'd gotten more handsome, too, though that seemed a bit more doubtful. But he was sure he hadn't gotten any younger. In fact, after reading Henrietta's manuscript, he felt about ten years older.

He wondered how many other people in Clearview had read the manuscript, or had heard Henrietta read it at one time or another. He wondered why Mildred Cramer hadn't mentioned it.

He didn't think that the manuscript could ever be published, but he wasn't absolutely certain. It had held his interest, all right, but would it interest a publisher in New York, someone who didn't know the characters involved? Rhodes wasn't sure.

And was there a motive for a real-life murder in the book? Rhodes wasn't sure about that, either, but if Vernell had read it, there certainly might be. The character of Bernell Kidsey, revealed in numerous flashbacks, was entirely reprehensible, without a single redeeming feature. She was a low, scheming liar, who wouldn't hesitate to destroy lifelong friends if doing so would help her get a book published.

And then there was Jeanne Arnot. Rhodes was pretty sure she hadn't seen the manuscript, but someone might have told her about it. The agent in the book, Jane Arnold, was even worse than Bernell, if that was possible. She used writers and editors like puppets and cut their strings when she was through with them, either that or left them to dangle helplessly without their puppet master to manipulate them. And she was having a passionate secret affair with Jerry Dan Gosling, a famous male cover model who was using her in his attempt to become the cover boy for every historical romance that was published.

There were several other people who didn't come off so well, too, including a well-known writer named Corrinna Bayer, who bore a powerful physical resemblance to Serena Thayer, though Rhodes hoped her personal qualities were different. She had quite a temper in the book, and she was sleeping with Jerry Dan Gosling in the hope that he would insist on doing her covers to the exclusion of all others.

Jerry Dan's motives were no better. He was sleeping with every writer and agent he could, his motive being a not-so-secret desire to appear on the cover of every historical romance novel published, a desire that didn't sit too well with Corrinna Bayer.

Another character, a fiery redhead named Lorraine Denbow, came off somewhat better. She was pursued by men, but she always fended them off until they married her. She'd been married quite often.

There were some pretty sexy passages, and the book reminded Rhodes vaguely of something he'd read many years ago by someone named Harold Robbins. Lots of intrigue, plenty of sex. Maybe that's what people wanted in mystery novels these days.

Rhodes went back into the office and put the manuscript back in the box. He wondered what Ruth Grady would make of it. He decided to give it to her and let her read it later that day.

But first he was going back to Obert and have a look in those trees. He was going to let Billy Quentin know he was there, though. He didn't want to take a chance with that shotgun.

Rhodes stopped for lunch on the way to Obert. There was a Pizza Hut on the road out of town, and Rhodes hadn't had a pizza in a long time, not unless he counted the vegetarian pizzas that Ivy made with no-fat cheese and no-fat pizza sauce. And Rhodes definitely didn't count those at all. He was in the mood for some stringy mozzarella and some pepperoni that wasn't made out of tofu.

But, telling himself that he was doing the virtuous thing, he didn't order a large pizza, or even a medium. He got the personal-size pan pizza, which he was certain had only a minimal number of calories and fat grams.

He had a Dr Pepper, too, but that didn't really count because it was served over ice in a paper cup. It didn't taste so much like a Dr Pepper as it did a glass of fizzy brown water that had been soaking in cardboard for weeks. Rhodes wouldn't have ordered one at all if he'd thought he could get a Dr Pepper in a plastic bottle, or even a can, but the Pizza Hut didn't work that way.

After he'd eaten, which didn't take long, Rhodes drove to Obert. He went past the college campus and straight down the hill to Billy Quentin's house. Quentin wasn't at home, so Rhodes left a note on his front door while lovable furry old Grover barked and barked.

Rhodes had no idea what he was looking for, but he stayed in the woods for more than two hours, poring over the ground and hoping to find something that might prove to be a tie-in to the murder, or at least something that might help him identify the woman that Mrs. Appleby and Claude had seen.

He hadn't found anything of interest and was about to give up when something caught his eye. He walked over to a clump of leaves and stooped down to pick up what appeared to be a piece of cloth, which is exactly what it was. But it was more than that, too. It was a black crew sock.

Rhodes got a stick off the ground and picked up the sock with it. Then he tried to figure out what it meant.

A naked woman in black crew socks? Rhodes didn't think so. Besides, how could the sock have come off her foot?

And did black crew socks go with red bikini panties? Rhodes

didn't have much fashion sense, but crew socks and bikini panties seemed an odd combination.

The sock hadn't been there long, however. It had been right on top of the ground, and it was fairly clean, with only a leaf clinging to it.

Rhodes looked around for signs that someone had been there, and he found them: crushed leaves, a broken twig. But no clearly defined footprints, and no other clues.

Rhodes had brought a couple of paper bags in his back pocket. He got one out and dropped the sock in it. He didn't know what value it might have, but he was pretty sure it was somehow connected to everything that had happened. He'd take it back to the jail and put it in the evidence locker until he figured it out.

If he ever did.

Billy Quentin still wasn't at home, so Rhodes couldn't ask him if he'd lost any socks. Claude and Clyde were at work, but Mrs. Appleby was sitting in her living room watching Sally Jessie Raphael's audience taunt a young man who had apparently been sleeping with his much older stepmother.

"The world is full of trash," Mrs. Applebly observed, shaking her head.

Rhodes didn't comment. He just asked if either Claude or Clyde might be missing a sock.

"A sock?"

"A black one," Rhodes said. "Thick cotton."

"They don't like thick socks," Mrs. Appleby said. "They like those thin ones that have a lot of elastic in them and stay up good. They don't even own any thick ones. Why?"

"Somebody lost one back in the trees," Rhodes said.

"You think it was that naked woman?"

Rhodes said that he doubted it.

Mrs. Appleby did, too. "She wasn't wearing any socks that I could see. Just those panties."

Rhodes thanked her for her help and left.

* * *

There was a session in progress when Rhodes stopped at the college, so he sat out on the porch of the main building and talked to Chatterton.

"What are they talking about?" Rhodes asked.

"How to write a synopsis," Chatterton said. "It's very important to be able to write a good synopsis, they tell me. They even have contests to see who can write the best one. They charge a fee to enter and get some writer to be the judge. That's how they help pay for conferences like this one."

Rhodes didn't quite understand why anyone would want to write a synopsis.

"Why not just write the whole book?" he asked.

Chatterton explained that professionals never wrote a book unless they were certain that it would sell. Only beginners wrote the whole book.

"You seem to know a lot about it," Rhodes said. "Why aren't you attending any of the sessions?"

"Because I don't want to write a book. I might be the only person here who doesn't, though."

"What about Terry Don Coslin?"

"Oh, he's going to all the sessions. I believe he has a contract to write a historical romance. It's supposed to be a very lucrative deal."

"You're kidding."

"Oh, no. It was in all the papers. 'Model Turns Author.' That sort of thing."

"He's actually going to write a book?"

Chatterton laughed. "Of course not. You don't really believe that celebrities write their own books, do you?"

Rhodes said that he'd never thought about it.

"Well, they don't. Or maybe some of them do, but most of them don't. They don't have time. They're too busy being celebrities. So someone else writes the book, and the celebrity's name goes on the cover. It's supposed to help sales. And some celebrities like to keep up the illusion that they're the real authors. Mr. Coslin's doing that by attending the sessions."

"Does the big name on the cover help sales?"

"I have no idea. And in this case, it should be especially interesting. Women who read romance novels don't generally buy books written by men."

"Why not?"

"I suppose they think men don't know anything about romance."

Rhodes decided it was time to change the subject.

"How's Terry Don as a roommate?" he asked.

"Very quiet," Chatterton said. "I hardly heard a peep out of him all night."

"Did you know he went wandering around down the hill?"

"He said something about that at breakfast this morning. A very amusing story, except for the part about the gunshots."

"Maybe he can use it in his novel," Rhodes said.

11
▼

VERNELL LINDSEY DIDN'T WANT TO TALK TO RHODES IN THE least. She told him that there was one more session, and she was going to attend it.

"It's about writing a screenplay," she told Rhodes. "I can't miss it."

Rhodes said he thought she could.

"It's about murder," he said.

"I don't care if it is. I have to be at that session. It could be important to my career."

"Your career doesn't matter right now," Rhodes said. "Henrietta does."

"Henrietta's dead."

They were standing in the big hallway of the main building, where most of the people attending the conference were loitering, waiting for the next session. Vernell's voice was shrill, and people turned to look at them.

"That's why she matters," Rhodes said. "Let's go outside where we can talk without everyone looking over our shoulders."

Vernell seemed to realize for the first time that Rhodes meant what he said and that he wasn't going away.

"Oh, all right," she said sulkily.

They went out onto the porch. Chatterton took a look at Rhodes's face and stood up.

"I think I'll go check the dormitory," he said, and left.

"Let's get it over with," Vernell said. "What do you want?"

Rhodes wanted a lot of things, but he didn't think Vernell would be much help with most of them. He said, "I want to ask you about a book."

"A book? Are you joking?"

"I wish I was," Rhodes said. "It's not a published book. It's a manuscript called *A Romantic Way to Die*."

"Never heard of it," Vernell said, not very convincingly.

"I think you have," Rhodes said. "You might as well tell the truth because I'm going to be asking a lot of other people about it."

Vernell thought about that for a full minute. Then she said, "All right. I've heard of it, but I've never seen it. For all I know, it doesn't even exist."

"It exists all right," Rhodes told her. "Where'd you hear about it?"

"From Henrietta," Vernell said. "She took great pleasure in telling me all about it. She said that before long, everybody in Clearview and the whole world was going to know what kind of bitch I am."

"What did she mean by that?"

"I assume she thought the book would be published. She always did have a high opinion of her own writing. Much too high an opinion, I might add. She couldn't write a publishable page, much less a publishable book."

"It's not *that* bad."

"You've read it?"

"Yes."

"Well, you're not the only one. I heard about it from other people, too."

"Who?"

"Lorene Winslow, for one. She was practically Henrietta's only friend. She'd read it. She thought it was funny."

Rhodes hadn't thought so, but he could see how Lorene might get that impression.

"Has Jeanne Arnot read it?"

"I don't know. Why?"

"I just wondered. If Henrietta was planning to sell it, she'd need an agent."

"Not Jeanne. She turned down three of Henrietta's manuscripts. Henrietta hated her."

Somehow that didn't come as much of a surprise to Rhodes.

"What did Henrietta have against Terry Don?" he asked.

"You mean you don't know?"

"If I knew, I wouldn't ask."

"You don't have to get huffy. I guess I just took it for granted that the sheriff knew everything that went on in the county."

"Not this sheriff," Rhodes said.

"There's no real reason why you should have known," Vernell said. "It was all a long time ago. Henrietta and Terry Don dated in high school. And she got the idea that he was going to marry her when they graduated. It was sort of like her idea that she was going to be a writer, I guess, something that was mostly in her head."

All that was news to Rhodes, and it slightly changed the way he'd been looking at things.

"Serena Thayer's in the book, too," he said.

"Oh, my God. What does it say?"

Rhodes told her.

"I hope Serena hasn't heard that. She'd kill Henrietta."

Rhodes started to remind Vernell that someone already had, but Vernell thought of it for herself.

"Oh, my God," she said again. "Serena has a terrible temper. Everyone knows about it, but nobody ever talks about it."

Rhodes remembered a few incidents from the book. One episode described Serena's attack on a hotel maid with a high-heeled shoe. The maid's crime had been her failure to put a chocolate mint on Serena's pillow.

"Henrietta talked about it," Rhodes said. "What did she have against Serena?"

"Terry Don," Vernell said. "Everyone knows—" She stopped and looked at Rhodes. "Well, not everyone. But it was an open secret that Serena had a thing for Terry Don. Of course Terry Don is used to that sort of thing. I mean, look at him."

Rhodes said he'd rather not, and he didn't mention the other things that Henrietta had said about Terry Don. Probably everybody knew, anyway.

Vernell looked thoughtful. "There was a rumor that there's more to Serena and Terry Don than just a physical attraction. Someone said that she wanted him to acknowledge that they were having an affair and then appear on her book covers exclusively."

"What would be the purpose in that?" Rhodes asked.

"It's very romantic, don't you think?"

Rhodes wasn't sure. Probably it was like Chatterton had said: men didn't know anything about romance.

"And besides," Vernell continued, "it would drive the other writers completely crazy if it worked. Serena's sales would double. Maybe triple. Everyone would hate her even more than they do now."

"They hate her?" Rhodes said.

"Envy her is more like it. She's very attractive, she sells lots of books, and every one she writes sells better than the last one. She's going to be big."

"But not if Henrietta's book is published. People would see another side of her."

"Everyone in the business already sees that side," Vernell said. "And I hope you don't think Serena killed Henrietta because of that manuscript. That's crazy. And I certainly hope you don't think I killed her. I know we weren't very good friends, but—"

"She thought you stole her idea," Rhodes said. "If you did, that would be a motive."

Vernell gave Rhodes an exasperated look.

"I never stole anything from anyone. Henrietta's book was terrible. Ask anyone who's read part of the manuscript and see what they tell you. She was just looking for someone to blame for her failure. Writers are like that."

Rhodes didn't know what Vernell was talking about, so she enlightened him.

"When a manuscript doesn't sell, it's never the writer's fault," Vernell said. "It's always the editor's fault, or the agent's fault. Or in Henrietta's case, my fault. People just don't like to admit that they might not have the talent to write a publishable book."

"So you were just a convenient target for her frustrations," Rhodes said. "There was nothing personal in it."

"That's it. Besides, I was in my room when she was killed. You heard what Carrie said."

"I heard," Rhodes said.

"Good. Now can I go to the meeting? I've probably missed half of it already."

She turned toward the door, and Rhodes said, "Speaking of something personal, maybe you heard about the contest the radio station was supposed to be running."

Vernell was reaching out for the door, but she dropped her hand and turned back to Rhodes.

"I heard about it," she said.

"Who told you?" Rhodes asked.

Vernell hesitated and dropped her eyes. Rhodes could tell she didn't want to answer the question.

"It would be easy for me to find out," he said.

Vernell looked up at him.

"All right, if you must know. Henrietta told me. That was a mean and spiteful trick, but she thought it was funny."

"The people she called didn't."

"No, but that just goes to show how stupid Henrietta was. From what I hear, the people she called got mad at the K-Vue, not at me."

"And it didn't bother you in the least, I guess," Rhodes said.

Vernell stared at him defiantly.

"No, it didn't. Like I said, it was just a stupid practical joke, and it didn't work. Now can I go to the meeting?"

Rhodes told her to go ahead. He had plenty to think about, and he wanted to get back to town and talk to Ruth Grady about her crime-scene investigation. And if Dr. White had done an autopsy on Henrietta, Rhodes wanted to know the results.

He was about halfway to his car when he saw Chatterton leave the president's house and head for the dormitory, which was only a few yards away. For some reason Rhodes wondered about Chatterton's story of the previous evening. He'd claimed that he'd been in the dormitory, but no one had backed him up. Rhodes would have called Vernell back to ask her if she'd seen him, but she'd already disappeared inside the main building.

Rhodes decided he'd ask Vernell another time. If he went into the meeting and tried to get her out, she'd probably cause a riot. It wouldn't be worth the trouble.

But Chatterton was a different story. Rhodes drove around to the dorm and went inside, where Chatterton was looking around the lounge area.

"I just wanted to tell you that I'd be back this evening," Rhodes said. "I have some more questions for everyone."

"I'll let them know," Chatterton said. "There won't be another session tonight, but we'll all be having dinner together at seven."

"I'll be by around eight, then," Rhodes said. "I hope you have a vegetarian meal this time."

"Don't worry," Chatterton said. "I thought that Ms. Thayer was going to get violent last night. I had to call the Round-Up several times this morning to make sure that things would be all right at lunch."

"And were they?"

"Yes, thank goodness. It wasn't easy, though."

Rhodes was sure it hadn't been. Potatoes were the only vegetable the Round-Up served with any regularity.

"I hope there wasn't any problem with breakfast," he said.

"I managed to drive to Clearview and get some fruit," Chatterton said. "I didn't want a repeat of last evening."

"I don't blame you," Rhodes said.

"Oh, I wasn't talking about the murder. I certainly wouldn't want that, but I wouldn't want another scene like the one Ms. Thayer caused, either. Not that there's any comparison."

"She must have quite a temper," Rhodes said.

"That's putting it mildly. Some of the women know her, and they weren't too disturbed. But some of the others were shocked. For that matter, so was I."

Nothing people did surprised Rhodes much anymore, but he didn't tell Chatterton that. He didn't want to seem cynical. So he just said, "I'll see you later," and left.

12
▼

When Rhodes got back to the jail, Ruth was there, talking to Hack about Miz McGee, the woman he'd been dating for a while. Though Hack didn't look it, he was in his seventies. But he was still quite the ladies' man, at least to hear him tell it.

"Last night we rented this video called *The Talented Mr. Ripley*," he was saying when Rhodes walked in. "You ever hear of it?"

Ruth said that she had. Rhodes hadn't, but then he wasn't exactly up-to-date when it came to movies. The kind he liked were the ones that used to be shown on late-night television shows sponsored by insurance companies that sold auto insurance to people even if their driving records were terrible, lawyers who appealed to accident victims or people who had workman's comp cases, and used-car dealers who would extend credit to mass murderers.

"It was kind of an interestin' movie," Hack said. "It happened in Italy, and it had some skinny blond woman in it. And there was a guy who was killin' people off one right after the other.

If those Italian cops were half as smart as our sheriff, they'd have arrested that guy before the movie was half over, but they were sort of slow. Come to think of it, so was the movie. Miz McGee went to sleep sometime in the first hour or so. I lasted the whole thing, though. I believe in gettin' my money's worth when I rent a video, even if it kills me."

"Speaking of killing people," Rhodes said, "what about that autopsy report?"

"Dr. White sent it over," Ruth said. "I put it on your desk. Things happened pretty much the way we figured. Henrietta was killed when she fell and hit her head on the sharp corner of that dresser."

"And had there been a fight?"

"Yes. There were marks on Henrietta's wrists where someone had held her."

"Fingernail scrapings?" Rhodes asked.

"No. Whoever was struggling with her got hold of her wrists before getting scratched."

"Too bad," Rhodes said, though he wasn't surprised. No one at the conference had had any visible scratches. "Did you find anything in the room that might help us?"

"There were plenty of fingerprints," Ruth said. "They were all over the place, but I'd be willing to bet they all belong to Henrietta or Lorene Winslow. There were some smudges on the window screen, but nothing that would help."

"How many criminals you ever hear of that got caught by fingerprints?" Hack asked.

"None," Ruth said. "But that doesn't mean there haven't been any."

"Hah," Hack said, and smiled a superior smile.

"So we're going to have to do it the hard way," Rhodes said.

"Don't we always?" Ruth said.

"At least this time nobody's shooting at us," Rhodes said,

recalling a recent case that had found him and Ruth at a cemetery being fired on with automatic weapons.

"Not yet, anyway," Hack said.

"I don't think any of those romance writers are carrying machine pistols," Rhodes told him.

"Some of 'em might surprise you."

Rhodes agreed that anything was possible and asked if anything had happened during the day.

"Nothin' you need to worry about," Hack said. "Just the usual stuff."

"Good," Rhodes said. "I'm going home, and then I'll be going back to Obert around eight."

He was almost to the door when the telephone rang. He had a feeling that he might be needed, so he stopped where he was while Hack answered.

Hack listened for a minute and said, "Lord a'mercy. Was it Henrietta's finger?"

Rhodes turned back. He knew now he wouldn't be going home for a while.

"Whose finger was it, then?" Hack asked.

Rhodes looked at Ruth, who shrugged.

"Lord a'mercy," Hack said again. "Poor old Larry. But I guess the good news is that he doesn't know about it, him bein' dead. The sheriff's right here. I'll tell him to get over there."

Hack hung up, and Rhodes said, "What's the problem?"

"Larry Tietz died the other day," Hack said.

"I heard about it," Rhodes said. "Heart attack, wasn't it?"

"That's what they say. Right there in the middle of a Lion's Club luncheon. Keeled over in his mashed potatoes. Which would've been a big disappointment to him if he'd known about it, since—"

"You said something about a finger," Rhodes said, to get things back on track.

"Yeah. He cut it off."

"Larry Tietz cut off his finger?" Ruth said. "But he's dead."

"*He* didn't cut it off. Somebody else did. He was tryin' to smoke it."

"Smoke it?" Rhodes said. "Don't tell me we have a cannibal on the loose."

"He's not on the loose," Hack said. "Clyde caught him."

Clyde Ballinger was the director of Ballinger's Funeral Home, and Rhodes had dealt with him many times in the past.

"And he's not a cannibal," Hack went on.

"So he didn't eat the finger?" Ruth said.

"He wasn't ever going to eat it," Hack told her. "He wasn't smokin' it like you'd smoke a ham. He was smokin' it like you'd smoke a cigar."

"I don't believe this," Ruth said. "You're trying to pull some kind of a joke on me."

"Not me," Hack said. "If anybody's jokin', it's Clyde Ballinger, and you can ask him all about it. Or you can, Sheriff. He asked for you."

"I'm going, too," Ruth said.

"Better hurry," Hack said. "Clyde was talking with his cell phone in one hand and his gun in the other."

"Come on," Rhodes told Ruth, but she was already at the door.

Ballinger's Funeral Home had once been one of the largest private homes in Clearview, with spacious grounds that included a swimming pool and tennis courts. The pool and courts were gone, and no one was living in the old house. All the people who spent the night there these days were dead. Ballinger had his offices in the brick servants' quarters out back, and his own home was next door.

Rhodes stopped in the back drive, and he and Ruth got out

of the car. It was dusk, and all the lights on the grounds were on, as well as all those inside the funeral home.

"I'm in here," Ballinger called from the back entrance to the building.

Ruth and Rhodes walked over to see Ballinger standing just inside the door. He was gripping a .38 pistol in both hands, pointing it through the open door of the embalming room.

"Come on in," Ballinger said, stepping into the embalming room so the officers could enter through the back door.

When they went inside, Rhodes looked into the embalming room. Somehow the place always bothered him, with its faint chemical smell and its easily cleaned porcelain and stainless steel glittering under the lights.

But what he noticed this time was the man who cowered in one corner. There was something on the floor in front of him, something that Rhodes was pretty sure was Larry Tietz's finger.

Ballinger stood off to one side, pointing his pistol at the man on the floor.

"I guess you're licensed to carry that thing," Rhodes said.

"Sure am," Ballinger told him. "Took the course and everything. Glad I did, too."

"You can put it up now," Rhodes said, and Ballinger stuck the .38 in the waistband of his pants.

"Is that Larry Tietz's finger?" Ruth said.

"It is," Ballinger said. "That young fella there cut it off. What's the penalty for mutilating a corpse?"

Rhodes said he wasn't sure. "But we don't have to worry about that. The judge will know."

The man on the floor looked up at them. He needed a haircut, and his clothes were dirty.

"Hack said he was trying to smoke the finger," Rhodes said. "Why?"

"Ask him," Ballinger said.

Rhodes did.

"It's not my fault," the man said. He nodded at Ballinger. "It's his."

"How's that?" Rhodes asked.

"The son of a bitch locked up his embalming fluid, that's how."

Rhodes looked at Ballinger.

"Well, he's right about that," Ballinger said. "I lock it up, all right. Because of people like him. I don't know how these rumors get started."

"What rumors?" Ruth asked.

"The ones about how smoking cigarettes soaked in embalming fluid can get you high," Ballinger said. "I had some calls from around the state. Some acquaintances told me they'd had some break-ins, so I started locking the fluid up in a closet. That's why he couldn't get at it."

"It doesn't explain the finger, though," Ruth said.

"Sure it does. He couldn't smoke a cigarette soaked in the stuff, so he decided that he'd try smoking a finger. I guess he thought there'd be plenty in there."

"Didn't work, though," the man said glumly. "Finger didn't draw worth a damn."

He stuck out a foot and nudged the finger, which rolled an inch or two across the tiled floor and then came to a stop. Rhodes noticed that the end that had been cut from the hand was scorched.

Ballinger rolled his eyes.

"You know I don't lock up until late," he said, "just in case someone wants to come in and view one of the clients. I was outside when I heard some noises in there. There wasn't supposed to be anyone here for a viewing, and my clients don't usually do much moving around. So I got the pistol and came over to check. That's when I saw our friend, sitting on the floor in here and sucking on that finger like it was a Dutch Masters. Do they make those anymore?"

Rhodes said he didn't know, though he thought cigars were a little more upscale than that these days.

"What are you going to do about the finger?" he asked.

"I don't know," Ballinger said. "Maybe I can reattach it. Will you need it for evidence?"

Rhodes said that he hoped not.

"Well, I'll see what I can do. But you better get that guy out of here before the family finds out what he did. Larry had a son who played college ball, guard or tackle or something in the line. He's gotten a little bit soft, but he's still big as a house. He'd kill anybody who chopped off his daddy's finger like that."

Rhodes looked down at the man in the corner and asked his name.

"Charlie. I don't want some big son of a bitch mad at me. I didn't mean any harm. I just wasn't thinking."

Now there was an understatement, Rhodes thought. He said, "All right, Charlie. You can get up now. We're going to take you to the jail. Nobody will bother you there."

Charlie stood up. He looked down at the finger and said, "All I wanted was a little smoke."

"You should have stuck to nicotine," Ruth said.

Charlie gave her a stern look.

"Don't encourage me," he said. "Don't you know that stuff'll kill you?"

13

▼

IT TOOK A WHILE TO GET CHARLIE BOOKED AND PRINTED, AND
when they'd finished it was almost time for Rhodes to go back
to Obert. He went home first, however, for a quick bite to eat
and to let Ivy know where he'd be.

Yancey bounced around Rhodes's heels like an animated dust
bunny while Rhodes sat at the kitchen table and ate what appeared to be a hot dog.

"You'd never know it was made from tofu, would you?" Ivy
said.

Rhodes said that he wouldn't, without adding that he wasn't
even sure what tofu was. He did know that the hot dog didn't
taste even vaguely like it had been made from meat, and he felt
a lot less guilty about having eaten the pizza for lunch.

After going outside for a quick romp around the yard with
Speedo, with Yancey yipping and yapping and rollicking right
along with them, Rhodes got back in the county car and headed
for Obert.

He arrived just in time for the fight.

*   *   *

He could hear shouting from inside the dormitory when he got out of the car. He'd taken only a couple of steps when the door sprang open and two women came tumbling out, locked together like they were involved in a Battle Royal on the WWF Smackdown. Rhodes tried to get out of the way, but they slammed into him, and the three of them went down in a pile on the damp grass, with Rhodes on the bottom.

He was aware of being punched, scratched, and kicked, but there wasn't much he could do about it, being pinned to the ground. He tried to get his hands underneath himself and push himself to his knees, but there was too much squirming and pummeling going on for him to get any leverage.

After a few seconds, however, some of the weight was pulled away, and he managed to roll to the side and stand up. He brushed himself off and saw that Carrie Logan, Belinda Marshall, and several other women were trying to hold Vernell Lindsey and Serena Thayer. The latter two women were straining toward each other like pit bulls on leashes, and they were slowly pulling Carrie and Belinda along while yelling crude insults that Rhodes thought were highly unlikely to appear in their novels.

The rest of the women from the dorm were jumping around and acting like cheerleaders. There was so much confusion that Rhodes couldn't tell who was there and who wasn't. He didn't know much about writers' conferences, but he was pretty sure the participants in this one were getting more than their money's worth. The general noise level was so high that he wished he'd been wearing earplugs. He tried to get someone's attention, but no one was paying him any mind. Everyone was too intent on the fight.

Someone touched Rhodes's arm from behind. It was Chatterton, who looked as if a vampire had drained all his blood. Or maybe it was just the light from the dormitory windows that made him look so pale.

"This is just terrible," Chatterton said. He had to put his mouth near Rhodes's head and shout to make himself heard. "You have to stop it."

Rhodes was about to say he'd give it a try when the two women broke free and lit into one another again. There was more screaming, hair-pulling, kicking, and even a little biting.

"Sheriff!" Chatterton said. "Do something!"

Rhodes stepped up behind Vernell and grabbed her right wrist just as she drew it back to give Serena a quick punch to the face.

For some reason he didn't suspect Vernell of having especially good reflexes, and she surprised him. She went with the flow, letting Rhodes pull her around, and at the end of the turn, she smacked him on the side of the head with a hard left fist, digging in with the knuckle.

Rhodes was jarred, but he didn't let go. He was sorry he hadn't when Serena jumped on Vernell's back. Serena locked her long legs around Vernell's waist, clamped her left arm around Vernell's throat, and grabbed a hank of hair with her right hand.

Vernell staggered backward, with Rhodes still holding her right wrist and following right along. He was afraid that if he let go, the two women would fall and hurt themselves.

Not that they weren't doing a pretty good job of that already. Serena was trying to yank Vernell's hair out by the roots, while Vernell was slamming her left elbow into various soft portions of Serena's anatomy.

What the heck, Rhodes thought, and let go.

The two women wobbled backward and bumped up against the dormitory wall, then fell to the grass. Rhodes walked over to them, surrounded by women yelling encouragement to the combatants.

Rhodes reached down, grabbed both Vernell's wrists, and

wrenched her away from Serena. Quite a bit of Vernell's hair remained behind, clutched in Serena's fist.

"Hold her," Rhodes said, shoving Vernell in Chatterton's general direction and turning to Serena, who was now up and shuffling toward him in a crouch, hands ready to claw out his eyes.

Rhodes wished for a police whistle again. Maybe he should start carrying one. He hoped that Jeanne Arnot would use hers, but she didn't.

Well, he had something that would make more noise than a whistle if his pistol hadn't dropped out of the holster in the first fall of the match. It hadn't. He drew it out and pointed it at a spot about three feet over Serena's head. She saw the gun and came to a sliding stop about a foot away from him.

"You wouldn't dare," she panted.

"Yes he would," Vernell shrieked from behind him. "Shoot her, Sheriff! Shoot her!"

Rhodes had no intention of shooting anyone, but he did want the fighting to stop. So he stood there, gun in hand, waiting for Serena to calm down. It took a while, but eventually her breathing slowed and she straightened her posture.

Her shirt was torn, her blond hair looked as if it had been restyled with a broken stick, and there were long scratches on her cheeks. She wouldn't be posing for any glamour shots for a while, Rhodes thought.

He holstered his pistol and turned around to have a look at Vernell. Chatterton had his hands clamped around her arms, and she was struggling to throw him off. Fortunately, he was stronger than he seemed.

Vernell looked even worse than Serena. Her hair was hanging in her face, which had been rubbed into the dirt, and there was something that might have been a spider clinging to her cheek. Rhodes thought it might be a false eyelash.

"What brought all this on?" Rhodes asked, and everyone started talking at once.

Rhodes got out his pistol again and fired it into the air twice. Things got very quiet.

"That's better," Rhodes said. "Let's just have one person talking at a time. Who knows how all this got started?"

No one said a word for a few seconds, and it was so quiet that Rhodes could hear Vernell's raspy breathing. Finally Chatterton spoke up.

"I'd tell you, Sheriff, but I don't know. I just sort of walked into it like you did."

"What about you, Ms. Arnot?" Rhodes said.

Jeanne Arnot was standing on the edge of the group watching the goings-on with an amused grin. She hadn't joined in the cheerleading as far as Rhodes could remember, but she seemed to be enjoying things now.

"I'm not sure," she said. "Vernell and Serena were talking, and all of a sudden they were at each other's throats. You'll have to ask them."

"That's right, Sheriff," Carrie Logan said. "It all happened pretty quickly. I don't think anybody knows what started it."

"Somebody does," Rhodes said. "I think Mr. Chatterton and I will take Ms. Lindsey and Ms. Thayer over to the president's house for a little conversation. The rest of you can go about your business."

Rhodes waited until the writers and prospective writers started to drift back into the dormitory. Then he took Serena's arm.

She shook him off and said, "I'll go. Just don't touch me."

"You can let go of me, too," Vernell told Chatterton. "I'm not going to run away."

"Good," Rhodes said. "Let's go."

They were about halfway there when something occurred to Rhodes, something he should have thought of earlier.

"Where's Terry Don Coslin?" he asked.

14

▼

NOBODY SEEMED TO KNOW WHERE TERRY DON WAS. IT BOTH-
ered Rhodes a little that Terry Don never seemed to be around
when things happened. Of course he'd been there when Billy
Quentin started shooting, but not when Henrietta died and not
when the fight broke out. Rhodes looked around the crowd to
see who else was missing.

"Where's Lorene Winslow?" he asked.

"Right here," Lorene said from the back of the crowd.

Rhodes couldn't tell whether she'd just walked up or whether
she'd been there all along.

"Have you seen Terry Don?" he asked her.

"I haven't seen him since dinner," Lorene said.

Neither, apparently, had anyone else.

"He ate at my table," Chatterton said. "I had to check on some
things, and when I got back he was gone. I assumed he went on
back to the president's house."

"I guess we'll find out when we get there, then," Rhodes said.
"Come on."

Chatterton took the lead. Rhodes waited until Vernell and

Serena had started walking, then fell in behind them.

"I think this is stupid," Serena said when they were halfway there. "I don't know why you want to question us about a private disagreement. It's none of your business."

"It's about a murder case," Rhodes told her. "That makes it my business."

"You don't know what it was about. You don't have a clue."

Rhodes supposed Serena was hoping Vernell would take the hint and keep her mouth shut. He didn't think it would work out like that, however.

When they got to the president's house, Chatterton went inside first. Rhodes and the two women waited on the porch. Chatterton was back in only a few seconds.

"There's no one in there," he said. "I don't know where Mr. Coslin could be."

"We'll worry about that later," Rhodes said. "Why don't you take Ms. Thayer into the kitchen. I'll question Ms. Lindsey in the living room."

Chatterton led Serena away, while Rhodes and Vernell got situated. Vernell sat in a chair, but Rhodes preferred to stand.

When Vernell was seated, Rhodes said, "Well?"

"Well, what?"

"Do you want to tell me what caused all the trouble, or are you going to let Ms. Thayer get her story on the record first?"

Vernell thought it over. If she'd considered keeping quiet, she changed her mind. She couldn't afford to have Serena giving an account that might make Serena look completely innocent.

"There's not really much of a story to tell," she said. "We were just talking."

"Not when I saw you," Rhodes said.

Vernell didn't say anything.

"Something started that fight," Rhodes said after a while. "I want to know what it was."

Vernell still didn't say anything. Rhodes decided to wait her out this time. He wouldn't talk if she didn't.

"It was about Terry Don," she said at last.

"What about him?"

"About what she was trying to do. You said you read Henrietta's book. Well, that part was true."

"Serena was really trying to get Terry Don to be on the covers of all her books?"

"Not just that. She wanted him on her covers and nobody else's."

Rhodes said he wasn't sure what was wrong with that.

"It was her methods," Vernell said. "It wasn't like people didn't know. Henrietta was just repeating what everybody else had already said."

"That Serena was sleeping with him," Rhodes said.

"Of course. And she was getting possessive. That didn't sit well with Terry Don. He wasn't a one-woman man."

"So I gathered from what I read."

"Writers are terrible gossips," Vernell said. "Even someone like Henrietta, who wasn't exactly an insider, knew about Terry Don."

"Did Serena know about Henrietta's manuscript?"

Vernell looked at the floor.

"Well?" Rhodes said.

"I might have mentioned it to her."

"Before the fight?"

"I guess you could say that."

"Do you want to be a little more specific about what you said and when you said it?"

"Not really."

"Try it anyway."

Vernell sighed, then said, "I told Serena she was a character in a book that Henrietta had written. It didn't seem to surprise her. I remember wondering if she'd heard about it from someone else. Anyway, I told her that I thought the character in the book was just like her. Only nicer."

"And then the fight started," Rhodes guessed.

"No. I should've let it go, but Serena smiled a smug little smile, and that made me mad. So I said that I thought Terry Don was too good for her."

"And that started things," Rhodes said.

"No. She just kept on smiling. So I said that I thought the book was right about her temper and that maybe she killed Henrietta because Terry Don still loved her. You know. From high school."

Rhodes waited.

"And that's when the fight started," Vernell said. "She said I was a lying witch, except she didn't say *witch,* and then maybe I slapped her."

"Maybe?"

"Okay, so there's no maybe. I slapped her. But she shouldn't have called me that. She slapped me back, and then things got a little out of hand."

"And that's the whole story."

"That's it. I'm totally embarrassed by the whole thing. I wouldn't blame anybody who wanted to get a refund and leave the conference. I'm sorry I ever tried to put it on in the first place. I should've known something bad would happen if Terry Don came back here. Henrietta never got over him, even if he did sleep with half the romance writers in America."

"That would be a lot," Rhodes said.

"Yes, but look at him. Can you blame women for being crazy about him?"

Rhodes just didn't get it. Maybe it was the hair. Or maybe it was those pecs. Or both.

"So there was nothing more to the fight than that," he said.

"That's all. You know what Serena's temper is like. You read the book."

"But you're the one who did the slapping," Rhodes pointed out.

Vernell was clearly insulted.

"What difference does that make? She's the one who started things."

Rhodes thought about it. Vernell had been the one to initiate the conversation. She was the one who hadn't stopped talking about Henrietta's book, even when Serena remained calm. She was even the one who'd struck the first blow. But she still seemed to believe that Serena was at fault.

Then Rhodes remembered what Vernell had told him about writers. They were always looking for someone to blame. Maybe that wasn't true, Rhodes thought. Maybe it was only Vernell who was like that.

"All right," he told her. "Thanks for your help. You can go on back to the dormitory now."

"What about Serena?"

"I'm going to talk to her, get her version of the story."

"What good will that do? She'll probably lie to you."

"I'll just have to take that chance," Rhodes said.

He waited until Vernell had left, then went back to the kitchen. Chatterton and Serena were sitting at the table, drinking something in tall green iced-tea glasses.

"Diet Dr Pepper," Chatterton said, holding up his glass. "Can I get you one?"

Rhodes repressed a shudder. It didn't matter how hard the advertisers worked to convince people that Diet Dr Pepper tasted just like the real thing. He knew better.

"No, thanks," he said. "Would you mind going into the living room? I'll just talk to Ms. Thayer in here."

Chatterton left, taking his Diet Dr Pepper with him, and

Rhodes sat at the table. Serena took a sip of her drink and looked at him over the rim of the glass.

"Why the formality?" she said. "You can call me Serena."

Her eyes seemed even bluer than Rhodes had remembered. Rhodes supposed she hadn't had to work too hard to seduce Terry Don, if indeed he'd needed seducing, which seemed doubtful.

"In a murder investigation, you need a little formality," Rhodes said.

Serena smiled and pouted at the same time.

"Well, if that's the way you want it," she said. "What did Ms. Lindsey tell you about the fight?"

"I think I'd like to get your story before we discuss hers," Rhodes said.

"That's easy enough. Do you want the short version or the long one?"

"Try the short one."

"Okay. Vernell called me a slut and slapped me in the face. So I slapped her back. That made her crazy, and she tried to punch me. After that, I'm a little vague on the specifics."

It was short, all right, but it corresponded pretty well to what Vernell had said, except now it was Vernell doing the name-calling. And except for what had been left out.

"You forgot to mention that she accused you of murder," Rhodes said.

Serena smiled. "I knew she'd tell you that. She said I was jealous. But let me ask you a question, Sheriff. Do I look like a woman who'd be jealous of someone like Henrietta?"

She gave him a dazzling smile and widened those big blue eyes.

Rhodes smiled back, probably a lot less dazzlingly. His eyes weren't blue, either, so the effect was totally different.

He said, "No, you don't. But then you don't look like a

woman who'd go crazy if a hotel maid left the chocolate off her pillow, either."

Serena slammed her glass down on the table and stood up, her body rigid.

"That's a lie! You read that in that manuscript, didn't you!"

"Yes," Rhodes said. "Did you?"

Serena's face fell, and she sat limply back down.

"You tricked me," she said.

Rhodes resisted the urge to say it had been easy.

"When did you read it?" he asked.

"I don't remember. Terry Don showed it to me."

"Terry Don had a copy?"

"Of course. You may not know it, but Henrietta still loved him. She started writing him when he became famous. He told me all about her, the woman who'd never gotten over her high-school crush. When she sent him the manuscript, he let me read it."

"What did he think about it?"

"He thought it was funny."

"He didn't come off too well in it," Rhodes said.

"Why? Because he was supposedly sleeping with all those writers and agents? There were already stories going around about that, and they just enhanced his reputation. Probably got him a few more covers, if that's possible."

"According to the book he wanted to be on the cover of every historical romance novel that was published."

"That was Henrietta's idea. Terry Don would have settled for just a few more covers and a little more money. Not that he'd have objected to a lot more money."

Rhodes returned to his original question.

"And you weren't jealous of him?"

"No. Henrietta's book was a combination of gossip and her own imagination. That part was just her imagination."

"So naturally you didn't kill her."

"Of course not. I have too much to live for. I'm going to be the next Sandra Brown."

Rhodes actually knew who Sandra Brown was, mainly because she was from Texas. In fact, he remembered her from the time she'd done the weather on some Dallas TV station. He'd even seen her a couple of times. But she hadn't stuck with the weather. She'd turned her hand to romance novels and become a huge success. These days she was writing book after book that wound up on the best-seller lists.

"And Terry Don couldn't help you become the next Sandra Brown?" Rhodes said.

"Nobody can help you do something like that. You have to be good, which I am, and you have to have a little luck. I've always been lucky. You watch. I'll be on the best-seller lists before you know it."

Rhodes looked in those blue eyes and almost believed her.

15

▼

Rhodes sat in the kitchen after Serena had left and thought things over. Serena and Jeanne Arnot had sort of alibied one another in Henrietta's murder, but only sort of. He'd have to look into that. And while Serena didn't look like a killer, at least not like any killer Rhodes had ever seen, she certainly had a terrible temper, a fact that Rhodes supposed was ironic, considering her name. Serena was far from serene, at least some of the time, and it seemed to Rhodes that Henrietta's death could have resulted from sudden anger and a push at the wrong time. Or the right time. But Serena wasn't the only one with a temper. Vernell could hardly be described as mild-mannered.

Rhodes also wondered about Jeanne Arnot. Earlier he'd thought it unlikely that she'd read Henrietta's manuscript, but if Serena had, maybe Jeanne had as well. He'd ask her later. If she had, she might have thought that her reputation would be ruined if the book were published. That would be a motive for murder right there if the stories about how much money Jeanne was making were true.

Rhodes wondered if someone from New York might ever be

taken with the idea to stroll naked through the Texas countryside at night. Jeanne Arnot looked to him as if she'd be more at home using her police whistle to hail a taxi in Manhattan than she would out under the stars in Obert, Texas, but someone had been roaming around out there in the buff when Henrietta was killed unless the Applebys had been lying, and they had no reason to do that. Billy Quentin had heard someone, too, though he was convinced it wasn't a naked woman.

And then there was Terry Don Coslin. Where was he? Maybe that was what Rhodes needed to find out first. He got up and went into the living room. He was just about to open the door when it burst in on him and Chatterton came through.

"I can't find him anywhere!" Chatterton said.

"Who?" Rhodes asked.

"Coslin. I walked Vernell—Ms. Lindsey—back to the dormitory, and while I was there I looked around for him. He wasn't there. Nobody knows where he is. Nobody's seen him since dinner."

Rhodes wondered briefly if Terry Don might be wandering around on the hill, but he decided that wasn't the case since he hadn't heard any shotgun blasts.

"Could he still be in the main building?" Rhodes asked.

"Maybe. I don't know what he'd be doing over there, but I'll go and have a look."

"I'll go with you," Rhodes said.

Although the caterers had finished cleaning up and left, the old building wasn't completely dark. There was a weak lightbulb glowing on the porch. A few moths fluttered around it, making fragmentary shadows on the wall. There was dim light somewhere inside.

The door was open, and Chatterton went right on through. He flipped a switch on the wall, and the whole bottom floor lit up.

"Should we call him?" he asked.

"Why not?" Rhodes said, and they did.

They got no response, and Chatterton said, "I guess he's not here, either."

"What about the second floor?" Rhodes asked.

He had been on the second floor before, and also on the third floor, which was where he'd found the body of Simon Graham, the book dealer who'd had the idea of restoring the college in the first place.

"There's nothing upstairs," Chatterton said. "There'd been a little work done up there when I took the place over, but nothing much had been accomplished. I took care of the missing windowpanes, and I might have something more done later, but right now this floor gives me all the space I need. So there wouldn't be any reason for anyone to go upstairs."

Just as Chatterton finished speaking, Rhodes heard a noise. Chatterton heard it, too.

"That came from upstairs," Rhodes pointed out.

"Probably just a mouse," Chatterton said. "But don't tell that to any of the writers." He laughed. "I wouldn't want them to think this place was infested with vermin. Besides, it might not have been a mouse or anything else alive. These old buildings make funny noises sometimes."

Rhodes remembered having seen a mouse or two in the upstairs on one of his previous visits. And, mouse or no mouse, he thought it would be a good idea to have a look.

"The top floors aren't wired for electricity," Chatterton told him.

"I'll get a flashlight from my car," Rhodes said. "You can wait here until I get back."

It didn't take long for him to go to his car and come back with the flashlight, but by the time he returned, Chatterton was gone.

*   *   *

Rhodes found the stairway and noticed one bit of remodeling that had been done. There was new floor covering on the stairs, replacing the worn and dusty green carpet that had been there the last time Rhodes had climbed them. Rhodes went on up to the top, and found Chatterton standing there in the semidarkness.

"I thought I told you to wait," Rhodes said.

"I couldn't," Chatterton said. "I had to come up here and see if there was anyone around."

"You couldn't see much without a light."

There was a twilight kind of glow around them, coming from the lighting on the first floor, but Rhodes couldn't see far into the dusty darkness.

"I tried calling again," Chatterton said. "I didn't get an answer."

Rhodes shined the light into the big open space and moved it around. There wasn't much to see other than a few boards lying on the floor and the dust motes that floated through the flashlight's beam. No mice, no sign of Coslin.

"Let's go on up to the third floor," he said.

The light from the first floor didn't help much at all as they climbed upward, so Rhodes led the way with his flashlight. When he arrived at the top of the stairs, he called Terry Don's name.

The top floor had once housed the college's chapel in one big room, which was now entirely empty. Rhodes's voice echoed off the bare walls and uncovered windows. Nobody answered him, and the light didn't reveal anything except more emptiness, a dilapidated stepladder, and a few old paint cans. A brush lay on top of one of them, its bristles stiffened by a thick coat of white paint.

Rhodes was about to turn and go back down the stairs when

he noticed something. He shined his light across the room again, and it lit up a broken window.

"I thought you'd replaced the missing panes," Rhodes said. "What happened over there?"

Chatterton said he didn't know.

"I thought everything was in pretty good shape," he said. "That window couldn't have been broken long or there'd be birds roosting in here."

Rhodes shined the light up at the open rafters, thinking that maybe a bird had made the noise he'd heard, though he was pretty sure now that it had been nothing but the creaking of the building as the old wood and stones shifted slightly. As if to confirm Rhodes's thought, there was another noise from up in the rafters, sort of a creaky sigh.

Rhodes pointed the flashlight beam upward. A bit of dust drifted down, but the light showed no sign that any birds had been roosting there, not for a long time at any rate.

Rhodes turned the light to the floor, trying to see if there were footprints in the dust. He couldn't make them out if they were there.

"I'm going over to the window and have a look," he said. "This time, you stay put."

Chatterton nodded, and Rhodes walked around the edge of the room, not wanting to disturb any footprints if they existed.

When he got to the window, he looked it over. The ceilings in the room were quite high, ten or twelve feet, the way ceilings had been in the time when the building had been constructed, and the windows were also quite tall. Each one had two columns of three panes on the bottom and on the top. The panes were separated by wooden strips from which most of the paint had flaked away.

The strips that Rhodes was looking at were broken. There were shards of glass on the floor and the windowsill, and a few jagged pieces remained stuck around the edges of the frame.

"I don't see how that could've happened," Chatterton said at Rhodes's elbow.

Rhodes turned and said, "This is the second time you haven't stayed where I asked you to."

"But this is my building. Someone's been vandalizing it, maybe even breaking into it and doing some other kind of damage. I have a right to inspect it."

"Not if you're interfering with an investigation."

"What are you investigating?"

"That's what I'm about to find out, I'm afraid," Rhodes said.

He almost hated to do what logically came next, but there was no way to avoid it. Being as careful as he could not to destroy any possible clues, he leaned out the window and shined his light at the ground three stories below.

Someone lay very still down there, staring up at the starry night sky. A piece of glass by the body winked back at Rhodes when the light passed over it.

Rhodes couldn't make out the face of the person who was lying down there, but he was pretty sure he'd found Terry Don Coslin.

16

▼

"**W**HAT A WASTE," RUTH GRADY SAID, LOOKING DOWN AT THE body of Terry Don Coslin.

Rhodes privately agreed, though maybe not for the same reasons.

"I want you to go up to the third floor and see what you can find," he said. "I'll look here, and after the ambulance comes, I'll talk to the writers and have a look in his room."

"I have a fluorescent lantern in the car, but that might not be enough light."

"It'll have to do," Rhodes said. "We can come back in the daylight and go over things again."

He'd already called Hack and had him send Buddy Reynolds to talk to the caterers from the Round-Up. He wanted Buddy to find out if they'd seen anything. Hack had protested that some of them might be in bed. Rhodes had said he didn't care, though he didn't really think Buddy would learn much from them.

"What does it look like to you?" Ruth asked.

"I think Terry Don went up to the third floor with someone, got into a scuffle, and fell through the window," Rhodes said.

"Or, more likely, he was pushed. You can see a couple of cuts from the glass if you look close."

"Couldn't it have been an accident?"

"It could've been. But you don't really think it was, do you?"

"Not after what happened to Henrietta. Who would've been up there with him? And why?"

"That's what I'd like to know," Rhodes said.

Everyone in the dormitory seemed dumbstruck. Henrietta's murder hadn't seemed to touch them, maybe because most of them didn't like her. But Terry Don's death was a different story. The women all sat quietly, some of them crying, some of them twisting tissues in their hands, some of them just looking blankly at each other or at the walls.

"I can't believe something like this could happen," Jeanne Arnot said. "I don't know about the others, but I'm not staying here any longer. I'm going back to New York where it's safe to walk the streets."

Rhodes wasn't sure whether she was joking or not. If she was, it seemed like an odd time to be attempting humor.

"I'm afraid I can't let you leave," he said.

"What do you mean 'let me'? This was still a free country the last time I checked. I can go anywhere I please."

"Not when you're a suspect in a murder case."

There were gasps in the room.

"You have to be kidding," Jeanne said. "I can't possibly be a suspect. I'm a respected literary agent."

Having read Henrietta's manuscript, Rhodes was pretty sure that *respected* wasn't the right word, not if Henrietta had been anywhere near the truth about Jeanne's personality.

"I'm not kidding," he said. "I'm not trying to trample on your constitutional rights, but nobody's going anywhere until I say so.

You can go right on with your workshop if you want to, but you can't go back to New York."

"I don't see how we can go on with things," Vernell said. "Not after what's happened."

"That's up to you," Rhodes said. "But I'm going to want to talk to everyone about tonight. If you'll go to your rooms, I'll call you out one at a time."

Rhodes had long ago learned that eyewitnesses were the worst kind. Of all the people who had been at the dinner that evening, not a single one had noticed Terry Don's leaving, nor had anyone seen who might have left with him. Or so they all claimed.

Lorene Winslow swore that she hadn't seen or talked to Terry Don all evening, but she did have a few things to say.

"I wasn't at Terry Don's table," she said. "Why don't you ask Tom?"

"Chatterton?" Rhodes said.

"That's right. Tom. Terry Don was at his table. If anyone knows where Terry Don went, Tom should."

"He doesn't know."

"That's what he told you. But do you believe him?"

"Shouldn't I?"

"How much do you know about him and Vernell?"

Rhodes knew nothing at all about Vernell and Chatterton. It was becoming apparent to him that he was a long way out of the mainstream of gossip in Clearview.

"What should I know?" he asked.

"Well, for one thing they were becoming an item."

Rhodes couldn't remember the last time he'd heard any couple referred to as an *item*.

"That's how this whole writers' workshop came about," Lorene said. "Henrietta told me all about it."

"You and Henrietta must have been pretty good friends," Rhodes said. "Since you were roommates and all."

Lorene brushed her improbable red hair back with one hand and tucked it behind her ear.

"I'm not sure Henrietta had any friends," she said. "Sometimes I think she went out of her way to make enemies."

"You've read the manuscript," Rhodes said.

"Good guess, Sheriff."

"But she seemed to like the character named Lorraine. She didn't try to make an enemy of you."

"We knew each other for a long time. But that doesn't mean we were friends."

"Did she talk to you about Terry Don?"

"Sometimes. But we didn't spend much time alone here at the workshop. So she didn't reveal any of her girlish secrets."

"And she didn't mention who might have been dropping by to see her last night?"

"Not to me," Lorene said. "I might have walked right in on them if I'd gone back to the room. Maybe she wouldn't have died if I had. Too bad I was over talking to Claudia and Jan."

Rhodes noticed the reestablishment of Lorene's alibi, but he didn't remark on it. He just agreed with what she said and returned to what interested him.

"What did Henrietta tell you about Chatterton and Vernell?"

"That Vernell was using Tom to get this workshop put together. She couldn't afford to pay the writers and the agent if she had to rent the campus facilities, so she started working on Tom. Vernell's not bad-looking, you know, and before long, she had Tom convinced that he needed to host something here to get things off the ground. The publicity would be good for him, and she could guarantee the publicity."

"She's going to get that, all right," Rhodes said. "One murder was bad enough, but this one is going to bring in the big boys."

Lorene gave him a puzzled look.

"The big boys?" she said.

"The city papers," Rhodes said. "And the TV crews. If Terry Don was as famous as I think he was, there'll be trailers and satellite dishes all over this place by morning."

"He was as famous as you think he was," Lorene said. "He was even about to get a TV commercial."

Rhodes hadn't heard that, either.

"Did Henrietta tell you that?" he asked.

"No. Terry Don did. He was telling everybody. He thought it was going to be his stepping-stone to a series."

"What kind of series?"

"He didn't care. He would've settled for a guest shot on *Xena.*"

Who could blame him? Rhodes thought. But he didn't see why Vernell's relationship with Chatterton would have had anything to do with Terry Don.

"You read the manuscript, too, Sheriff. So you know what Terry Don was like."

"You mean—"

"Yes."

"Oh," Rhodes said.

Vernell was irate that Lorene had mentioned her relationship with Chatterton.

"That redheaded filly," Vernell said. "As many husbands as she's had, you'd think she wouldn't criticize anybody else."

"Two," Rhodes said. "That's not many."

"Who cares? She even married the same man twice. And divorced him twice."

Rhodes admitted that was interesting if not excessive.

"Would Terry Don have been jealous of you?" he asked.

Verneil's eyes flashed.

"What makes you ask that?"

"Well, knowing what Henrietta said about him in her manuscript, I thought he might have approached you."

" 'Approached.' That's one way of putting it."

"Did he?"

"Did he what?"

"Approach you?"

"If he did, that's my business. It certainly doesn't have anything to do with his death, or with Henrietta's for that matter."

"What about you and Chatterton?"

"What goes on between Tom and me, if anything does, is private. It has nothing to do with anybody else."

Rhodes decided to let it go for the moment. Maybe it would come to something later on, maybe not. He would wait and see.

Rhodes finished interviewing the women and went to the president's house to see Chatterton. Chatterton didn't mind talking about Vernell. He thought she was a lovely and creative woman.

"I'm proud to be associated with her," he said.

"In more ways than one," Rhodes added.

"I know what you're thinking," Chatterton said. "But you're wrong. Vernell and I have a business relationship, and I owe her a great deal. If it hadn't been for her, I might never have gotten this place off the ground."

"You're going to get some bad publicity after what's happened," Rhodes told him.

"I'm sure you've heard this line before, Sheriff. But I'll repeat it anyway: there's no such thing as bad publicity."

"Being arrested for murder might be the exception."

Chatterton's mouth didn't quite drop open, but his eyes widened and his hands fluttered.

"What do you mean by that?" he asked.

"I mean that you might have killed Terry Don out of jealousy. Did you know he'd made sexual advances toward Vernell?"

"Who told you that?"

"It's confidential," Rhodes said.

Chatterton's face was slowly turning red.

"It doesn't matter who told you," he said. "It's a lie."

"I don't think so, and I think you know better. And I think you have more than a business relationship with Vernell. The question is, did you see anyone go upstairs with Terry Don tonight?"

"No. Why would I notice something like that?"

"And you didn't go up there with him yourself?"

"Don't be stupid, Sheriff."

"Thanks for the advice," Rhodes said.

Rhodes sent Chatterton to the dormitory while he looked through Coslin's room. His talk with Chatterton had given the sheriff a couple of things to think about.

How far would a man go to get publicity for a struggling business venture? Rhodes was pretty sure that some men would kill for the kind of media coverage Chatterton's campus would be receiving, and Chatterton had an additional motive: jealousy, one of the classics. Chatterton might claim that he was involved with Vernell only in business dealings, but his body language and facial expression said something different.

The problem was that Chatterton and everyone else seemed to have been at the dormitory while the fight was going on. Rhodes thought back to what had happened. It was hard to remember who had been there when he arrived because of all the confusion. And he'd been flat on his face there for a while, not the best position to be in if you were trying to look at people's faces. Feet, maybe, but not faces.

Rhodes used Chatterton's telephone and called Hack.

"Have you heard anything from Buddy about the caterers?"

"They don't know a thing," Hack said. "They just cleared the tables and left. They brought all the dishes back to town so they could wash 'em in the dishwashers, so they were out of there in ten or fifteen minutes after the meal was over with."

"Nobody heard anything?" Rhodes said.

"Nothin' out of the ordinary. If Terry Don fell out of that window while they were there, he fell real quietlike. I woulda yelled, myself. How about you?"

"Me, too," Rhodes said.

17

▼

TERRY DON'S ROOM WAS NEAT AND ORDERLY. HIS SHIRTS AND pants were hung in the narrow closet, and sitting on the floor beneath them was a cloth duffel bag. In the room itself, there were no clothes flung on chair backs or lying on the floor. The bed was made, and there wasn't a single wrinkle on the bedspread.

There was a dresser against one wall and a low table beside the bed. An imitation Tiffany lamp sat on the table by a small clock radio. There was a book on top of the radio. Rhodes was amused to see that it was a mystery novel. Terry Don might like being a cover model for historical romances, but he wasn't very loyal in his choice of reading material. The title of the book was *Masquerade*. Rhodes wondered if that was a clue, though he was pretty sure it wasn't.

There was also a round glass ashtray on the table. It had been emptied, but there were streaks of ash in the bottom.

Rhodes looked in the wastebasket, but there were no cigarette butts. There was nothing else, either. The wastebasket had been emptied, if it had ever been used at all. Rhodes ran a finger across the bottom, but there was no trace of ash. He didn't find anything in the room or in the suitcase to indicate that Terry Don was a smoker. There was nothing in the bathroom, either, except for the shaving kit, and that contained only an electric razor, a small bottle of designer shaving lotion, a comb, a brush, a toothbrush, and a tube of extrawhitening toothpaste.

Rhodes came out of the bathroom and looked at the dresser. Sitting on top was a stack of paperback book covers. Rhodes walked over to the dresser and picked up the covers. He flipped through them and saw that they were all for historical romance novels. Every single one featured Terry Don on the cover. There was always a woman, too, but the focus was on Terry Don.

On some of the covers his hair was a bit longer than others, and it wasn't always exactly the same color. Sometimes the color of his eyes was changed, too, but on every cover a large expanse of his chest was exposed. Sometimes he was wearing a torn shirt, sometimes the shirt was simply unbuttoned, and sometimes he wasn't wearing a shirt at all. None of the poses had much appeal for Rhodes, but he was sure they must have appealed to women. Otherwise Terry Don wouldn't have had so much work. On the other hand, Rhodes thought, remembering what Henrietta had written, maybe he would have.

Rhodes counted the covers. There were sixteen of them, and from the information printed on the backs, Rhodes gathered that all the books were recent. Some of them hadn't even been pub-lished yet. Terry Don might not have achieved his ambition of appearing on the cover of every historical romance novel that came out, but Rhodes thought that he must have been getting close to it, unless there were a lot more romances being printed than Rhodes thought there were.

Rhodes looked at the authors' names. Serena Thayer was there, and so was Belinda Marshall. Rhodes wondered if Belinda had slept with Terry Don. He'd have to talk to her again.

He put the covers back on top of the dresser and opened the

top drawer. There was a tidy stack of underwear, or what Rhodes supposed was underwear. He was a Jockey shorts kind of guy himself, but he liked something that pretty much covered the territory. What Terry Don had worn would barely get the job done. And it came in different colors. Rhodes had never owned a pair of shorts that wasn't white. Terry Don had been a lot more sporty.

But not as far as his socks were concerned. There were a couple of pairs, both of them black, both of them made of thick cotton. Rhodes thought he'd seen a sock like that very recently.

He closed the dresser drawer and went back to the closet. Picking up the duffel bag, he carried it to the bed, set it down, and opened it. As he'd suspected it might, it contained Terry Don's laundry.

It's finally come to this, Rhodes thought as he dumped the rumpled clothing out on the bed. *I'm literally going through somebody's dirty laundry.*

Besides some more wildly colorful underwear and a shirt, there was another pair of black socks. Or Rhodes supposed it was a pair. There was a third sock, too, identical to the others. It would be almost impossible to say which two of the socks belonged together.

Rhodes fumbled through the clothes, looking for the fourth sock. He didn't find it, which was no surprise. He thought he knew where it was: in the evidence locker at the jail.

On his way out of the house, Rhodes couldn't resist having a look in Chatterton's room, as well. Chatterton hadn't given him permission, but Rhodes wasn't worried. He wasn't going to do a search, just glance around.

Chatterton's room was, if anything, even neater than Terry Don's had been. Rhodes could have bounced a quarter on the bedspread if he'd wanted to, and if he'd had a quarter.

Rhodes wasn't surprised. Chatterton struck him as someone who'd keep things in their places, though Terry Don hadn't. For just a second Rhodes was ashamed of himself for stereotyping Terry Don, but he got over it very quickly. He was probably just jealous of Terry Don's pecs, which weren't doing Terry Don much good anymore.

There was one thing about Chatterton's room that Rhodes hadn't been expecting. In one corner, turned to face the bed, was a thirteen-inch color TV set sitting on a little TV stand on wheels. And there was a remote control on a nightstand by the bed. Apparently Chatterton had one rule for his guests and one for himself.

Nothing unusual in that, Rhodes thought, and let himself out of the house.

18

▼

RHODES WENT OVER TO THE MAIN BUILDING TO SEE IF RUTH
had finished her investigation of the third floor. As he climbed
the stairs, pointing the flashlight ahead of him, he heard her
moving around on the floor above. The sounds were nothing like
the creaking of the rafters that he'd heard earlier.

The fluorescent lantern was sitting on a paint can, and it threw
long shadows on the walls. Ruth was putting something in a bag
when Rhodes asked how the investigation was coming along.

"Just about done," she said. "There wasn't much to find,
though."

"Fill me in."

"You can see a couple of places where somebody shuffled
through the dust, but there aren't any clear footprints. The dust
is really disturbed under the window, but you and Chatterton
probably had something to do with that when you were looking
out earlier."

"We were careful," Rhodes said, knowing that was true of
himself. He wasn't so sure of Chatterton, however. In fact, the
more he thought about it, the more he wondered about Chatter-

ton, who wouldn't stay where Rhodes told him to. Could he have been deliberately trying to mess up the crime scene?

"Let's say we didn't mess things up," he said. "What would you think happened?"

"I'd say there were two people up here and that one of them pushed the other one through the window. It would've been easy. See how low the window ledge is?"

Rhodes had already noticed. The ledge was no more than knee high. It would've been easy to push someone hard enough to make him lose his balance and topple backward, especially if the push came as a surprise.

"Why would anyone be up here?" Rhodes asked.

"That's an easy one," Ruth said. "They wanted somewhere to talk privately. This is about as private as you can get."

Rhodes agreed. It was private, but dusty. Even as he thought about the dust, Ruth sneezed. She pulled a tissue from her pocket and wiped her nose.

"The dust up here is pretty bad," she said, jamming the tissue back in her pocket. "Or haven't you noticed?"

"I was just thinking about it, but dust doesn't seem to bother me. What were you putting in the bag when I came up?"

"Fibers from cloth of some kind," Ruth said. "They were on the window glass."

She pointed to one of the jagged glass teeth still clinging to the frame.

"Right there," she said.

"Could be from Terry Don's shirt," Rhodes said.

"It probably is," Ruth agreed. "On the other hand, maybe whoever pushed him couldn't resist having a look."

"Right. We should be so lucky. Anything else?"

"No. I'll come back up here tomorrow and try again when the light's coming through the windows. You never know what might turn up."

That was true, Rhodes thought. He was quite familiar with

the idea that everyone at a crime scene left something behind and took something away. But he didn't think anything more would turn up here than had turned up in Henrietta's room.

"You can go on home," he told Ruth. "I'm going to stay for a while. Maybe something will come to me."

Which, the way things had been going, was about as likely as something turning up in the morning, he thought.

"It's getting late," Ruth pointed out.

Rhodes didn't need anyone to tell him that. His eyes were burning, a sure sign that he needed some sleep. Or that the dust was bothering him more than he thought.

"Leave the lantern," he said, handing her the flashlight. "I might need it."

Ruth took the flashlight and said, "I have some crime-scene tape. I can put it across the doorway if you want me to."

"Good idea," Rhodes said, though he was sure the tape wouldn't keep anyone out, any more that it would keep him in.

Ruth attached the tape to both sides of the doorframe, told Rhodes good night, and left. Rhodes watched the doorway as the flashlight beam gradually faded away as his deputy descended the stairs.

Rhodes spent the next few minutes holding the lantern and going over the floor near the window, but he didn't find anything that Ruth had missed. He hadn't really thought he would. Maybe he was turning into a pessimist.

He set the lantern back on the paint can and walked back over to the broken window to look outside. On a clear day from the top of Obert's Hill you could look out over the countryside and see for long distances. You couldn't see as far at night, of course, not even with the moon, but Rhodes could see over the tops of the trees behind Billy Quentin's house and down at the Appleby place. He could see the white gravel of the country road that ran in front of their houses until it disappeared in the heavier trees farther on. He could see the still shapes of cattle in one of the pastures, and he could even see the dog pen behind Billy Quentin's house. He couldn't see Grover, but he saw the dark outline of a wooden doghouse, and he figured Grover was asleep inside, maybe dreaming of chasing rabbits through the pasture or barking at squirrels in the trees.

He imagined two people standing in front of the window at just about dusk. There wouldn't be much light for them to see by, but they could see one another's faces, look in one another's eyes. He wondered what they'd seen there.

Rhodes walked away from the window and sat on a paint can near the doorway, thinking about all that had happened and trying to make some sense of it. He had the beginnings of an idea, but that was all. He needed more than that, not only because he wanted to find the killer but because he was going to be bombarded by the press the next day. He wouldn't be surprised if even some of the tabloid reporters turned up. Terry Don Coslin was just the kind of character they loved to write about.

Rhodes had never had to deal with much media pressure. There had been a reporter for K-Vue, Red Rogers, who'd been a bit of a problem, but Rogers wasn't around any longer, as Lawton had pointed out the other day. Rhodes had never been pestered much by the local paper. The Clearview *Herald* had never won any prizes for investigative reporting.

But this was going to be a very different kind of situation. Rhodes hoped he could deal with it.

Rhodes listened to the sounds that the building made. He'd become more aware of them now that he was expecting them, and the stillness of the big, empty room made it all the easier to hear them. The wind, which had been hardly noticeable earlier, was blowing out of the north now, and it was coming in through the broken window, making a noise of its own. Rhodes figured the weather would be cold by the next morning.

He forced himself to stop thinking about the weather and to concentrate on the murders. As he sat there and considered the different aspects of the case, one thing seemed clear to him: someone was lying. Maybe several someones.

That was to be expected, of course. People always lied to the law. He wasn't entirely sure why, except in the case of the guilty. They had a pretty good reason. But why did other people lie?

In this case there were probably any number of reasons. To protect a friend, maybe, or to gain some kind of advantage over someone else. If Rhodes could figure out the reasons, maybe he could figure out who the liar was. Or the liars.

Because he was sure there was lying going on. Someone had struggled with Henrietta, and it was almost certain that not all the women had been where they claimed to have been at the time Henrietta died. One of them had been in that room with her.

Or maybe Chatterton had. He'd told Rhodes that he was checking to see if all the guests had what they needed, but Rhodes didn't recall that anyone had backed up that story. It would have been easy enough for Chatterton, or anyone else for that matter, to have gone out the back door of the dorm and run back around to the front, mingle with the crowd, and later swear they'd been there all along.

Would anyone have seen Chatterton leaving Henrietta's room? Rhodes wondered.

Maybe not, he thought. The room was at the end of the hallway, only a step or two away from the door to the outside. Out one door, out another, and into the darkness. And then there was that displaced window screen. Getting out without being seen would have been easy for Chatterton.

And it would have been easy for any number of others, too. Rhodes was going to start the next morning by trying to break down everyone's alibi. He'd start with Chatterton, and then move on to the others.

He also wanted to talk to Belinda Marshall, since Terry Don had been on the cover of her book. He wondered whether they were involved, and if so, how much. If there was something going on between them, and there probably was if Rhodes wanted to believe Henrietta's version of what Terry Don was like, then Serena might have yet another reason to become upset with Terry Don.

But that meant Rhodes would have to prove that Serena was up on the third floor with Terry Don, and in the room with Henrietta.

Rhodes sighed. It was time for him to go home and get some sleep. Maybe he'd get lucky and figure out the answer in his dreams.

Right, he thought. *And while I'm at it, maybe I'll dream of all the numbers in next week's Texas Lotto game.*

He picked up the lantern and started to stand. As he did, the light reflected off something near the window. Rhodes couldn't tell what it was, but he could see that it was in a crack between two boards, which no doubt explained why Ruth Grady had missed it. She'd have had to shine the light on it just right to know it was there.

As soon as Rhodes stood up with the lantern, the sparkle from the floor winked out as if it had never been. But he'd marked the place pretty well with his eye, so he started across the floor to where he thought it was, the old boards creaking under his feet.

This floor of the building no longer looked like a college chapel. The pews had long since been removed, and the floor had never been refinished or even touched up. The building had shifted on its foundation over the years, and there were wide spaces between some of the planks, while some of them were jammed so tightly together that there wasn't room between them for anything, not even a hair.

When Rhodes got to the spot where he'd seen the momentary glint, no matter how he shined the light, he couldn't seem to make it reflect off anything at all. He knelt down and tried to make the light shine along the cracks, but the shadows were all wrong, and it didn't work.

He was about to try going back to the paint can and having another look from there when the floor creaked behind him. Before he could turn to look and see what had caused the noise, something whished through the air and hit him in the back of the head and then he couldn't see anything at all.

Rhodes came to with a mouthful of dust. He spit it out and tried to swallow. The back of his head hurt, and he needed to sneeze. Maybe he was allergic to dust after all. Or maybe it made a difference if you were lying in it.

Either the lantern was gone or someone had turned it off. It was very dark. But there was a bit of light coming in through the windows, and if someone had been hoping that Rhodes would stumble over a paint can and break his neck, well, there wasn't much chance of that. He could see well enough to avoid any obstacles.

He sat up and put his hand to the back of his head. There was the beginning of a knot back there, and his hand felt dampness, which meant that the skin had been broken. He didn't think he was going to bleed to death, however. He was just going to have a very tender noggin for a while.

He wondered why anyone would hit him. Had there been something there, after all, something that both he and Ruth had missed and that someone had come back to retrieve?

He thought about that sparkle in the crack of the floor. He'd better have another try at locating whatever it was that he'd seen.

He stood up. A dull pain throbbed through his head, but it wasn't any worse than getting hit by a rubber hammer. He stood still for a few seconds and the throbbing went away. The dull pain, however, did not.

The lantern was lying not far from a paint can. The can hadn't been there earlier, and Rhodes figured it was what had hit him in the head. Rhodes bent down to pick up the lantern. When he bent over, the throbbing came back.

The lantern rattled loosely. Something inside was broken, and the plastic lens was cracked. Rhodes set it down on the paint can and looked around the room as best he could in the dim light.

Nothing was there that hadn't been there before, and as far as Rhodes could tell without better lighting, nothing was missing, either. Of course he couldn't see whatever it was that had glittered in the crack of the floor. It might still be there, or it might not.

Rhodes went over to the window. The cold wind blew in his face, and he felt a little better. Not much, but a little. He looked out and saw the tops of the trees tossing in the wind, but aside from the movement there was nothing different from what he'd seen earlier.

He wondered again why he'd been hit.

Maybe someone just doesn't like me, he thought. *Or maybe someone didn't want me to find whatever was in that crack.*

Well, he wasn't going to find it now, not without a light. It was time to go home, take some aspirin for the throbbing, and get some rest. He could come back in the morning with Ruth and find the sparkling thingamajig.

He went over to the door and slipped under the crime-scene tape, which, just as he'd thought, had proved to be no barrier at all.

He was about halfway down the first flight of stairs, feeling his way along in the dark, when an explosion somewhere below him shook the walls of the building and made the floor jump under his feet.

Rhodes pitched forward into the darkness. He stuck out his hands, but there was nothing to brace them against, so he fell forward and tumbled ankles over elbows the rest of the way down the stairs.

19

▼

RHODES WAS DOWN BUT NOT OUT. HE LAY AT THE BOTTOM OF the stairway on the second floor and tried to move. His head hurt even more than it had before, but it wasn't throbbing this time. It just hurt with a steady ache. His back hurt, and his right shoulder hurt. His knees didn't feel too good, either. Aside from that, however, he was just dandy.

Dust and dirt from the high ceiling drifted down on his face, but he didn't feel much like brushing it off. Besides, he was going to need all his energy just to get up, which he thought might be a good idea, especially since he could smell smoke.

The trouble with his good idea, however, was that his legs didn't seem to want to cooperate. So he just lay on the floor and tried to decide what had happened to cause the smoke and the downstairs detonation, which were two things he didn't much like, having only recently been blown halfway across the county by an accidental explosion in an amateur meth lab.

The smoke was rolling up the stairs from the first floor, and Rhodes figured that the blowup had occurred in the kitchen, where there was probably a gas stove. If the kitchen was all electric, then maybe he was wrong, but right now he was betting on a big gas stove.

He wondered why he was worrying about a gas stove, one that most likely wasn't even there anymore, when he couldn't even stand up. He was sure that if he didn't stand up, he was going to be in real trouble. But he didn't seem to be as worried as he should have been.

He wondered if anyone had called the Obert Volunteer Fire Department, not that it would do much good if anyone had. The fire truck was around forty years old, and Rhodes wasn't sure the volunteers could even get it started. He didn't even know if there were any fire hydrants in Obert. If there were they probably weren't anywhere near the college.

He tried again to get up, and this time he was able to force himself into a sitting position with his back against the wall. The smoke was getting thicker, and Rhodes started hacking and coughing. He knew that wasn't a good sign, since smoke inhalation was the main cause of death in fires.

Maybe that wasn't so bad, though. If you were already dead from inhaling smoke, you wouldn't feel it when you burned up.

He thought about himself as a mound of charred flesh in the middle of a pile of rubble, which didn't bother him any more than anything else, and coughed some more. Tears ran down his cheeks from his stinging eyes.

He slid slowly down the wall until he was almost lying down. Only his aching head and shoulders, one of which still hurt, remained braced against the wall. His eyes and lungs were full of smoke, and he didn't think he was going to be able to move again.

Too bad, he thought. On the other hand, it would give the reporters a nice sidebar for their stories: *Handsome, Talented Cover Boy Dies in Fall.* That would be the headline. Then, in a little box that nobody would pay much attention to, something about *Sheriff Dies in Mysterious Fire.*

Not that there was anything mysterious about it. Turn on the gas, pitch a match in the room, and *boom!*

Rhodes heard something that sounded like footsteps pounding up the stairs below him. He couldn't imagine who it was. He didn't much care, either, but opened his eyes to have a look. The smoke was so thick that he couldn't really see anything, and his eyes hurt, so he closed them again.

"Sheriff!" someone yelled. "Come on, Sheriff! We got to get you out of here!"

Rhodes opened his eyes. Standing over him was someone who looked like a stagecoach robber from an old black-and-white western, with a bandana pulled up over the lower half of his face. Rhodes had no idea what a stagecoach robber would be doing on the second floor of the old main building, but he knew what his duty was.

"You're under arrest," Rhodes said.

The robber reached down and grabbed Rhodes under the armpits and tried to pull him to his feet. Rhodes wasn't much help. He didn't feel like moving.

"You gotta help me, Sheriff," the stagecoach robber said. "Try to stand up."

"You're under arrest," Rhodes said again, or thought he said. He wondered if he was really saying anything at all. Then he knew he must have been because the smoke made his throat hurt. Maybe the robber wasn't listening.

"Come on, Sheriff. Get your feet under you."

Rhodes knew that would be a good thing to do, but he didn't have the energy to try it. The robber jerked on his shoulders, which hurt the sore one.

"Help me out here," he said. "If you don't, we're gonna burn up like marshmallows in a campfire."

Rhodes wasn't fond of that idea. Marshmallows were cracked and runny when they burned. He struggled with his legs and finally got a little leverage. He began pushing himself up, and with the robber's help he finally got himself to his feet. His legs were shaky, but he was standing. More or less.

The robber threw Rhodes's arm over his shoulders and said, "Let's get outta here."

The robber started down the stairs to the first floor, with Rhodes hobbling along at his side. When they were about half-way down, Rhodes's right knee gave out, and he would have fallen forward and down if the robber hadn't steadied him.

"Hang on, Sheriff," the robber said. "Don't try to get ahead of me."

"Wasn't trying," Rhodes said, though he didn't think the robber heard him.

They arrived on the first floor after what seemed a very long time, and Rhodes could see the front door. He buzzard-hopped toward it, still hanging on to the robber, who was half dragging him along.

They burst through the door and out onto the porch. Rhodes would have stopped there, but the robber kept right on dragging him, and Rhodes didn't have any choice but to keep going. When they were about thirty yards from the building, the robber collapsed to the grass, and Rhodes went down beside him. Both of them lay there, breathing heavily.

There was a siren in the distance. The volunteers had gotten the old fire truck started after all, Rhodes thought.

The siren seemed to fade in and out, so Rhodes stopped listening to it. He concentrated on breathing instead. Taking a breath was a little like having a splintery stick stuck down his throat, but the air was so sweet and cool that he kept right on drinking it in. It made him cough, too, but he didn't mind. The air tasted too good.

The robber, who was lying on his back and taking deep, racking breaths, didn't seem to be having a much easier time of it. He was coughing some, too, and he hadn't taken off the handkerchief. He sucked it into his mouth every time he took a breath.

Rhodes rolled up on his side, reached over, and pulled off the robber's mask.

"Hey, Claude," Rhodes said.

"Hey, Sheriff," Claude said. "I guess you owe me one."

"We'll have to see about that," Rhodes said.

20

▼

"YOU SHOULD BE IN THE HOSPITAL," IVY SAID. "I GUESS YOU know that."

Rhodes looked at himself in the bathroom mirror. He looked pretty bad, all right. Not as bad as a marshmallow from the campfire, but still not exactly the picture of health. There was no use in denying it. But a good hot bath would get most of the soot off him.

It wouldn't do much for the knot on his head, however. Or the bruises on his arms, legs, shoulders, and probably other locations, considering the way he felt.

"You probably have a concussion," Ivy said. "Or worse."

She might be right about that, Rhodes thought. But what was a little concussion? Professional football players went right back into the game after sustaining a concussion. Most of the time they didn't even call it a concussion. They called it a "stinger" or something like that. And that's all he had. A little stinger.

"Hold up some fingers," he told Ivy.

Ivy made a vulgar gesture.

"Not like that," Rhodes said. "You should be ashamed of yourself."

"I was just checking you," Ivy said. "At least you can still see one finger."

Rhodes had never been sure whether the inability to count fingers was a real test for a concussion or not. He remembered that his high-school football coach would always hold up two fingers, and if a player could count them, the coach would put him back in the game. But then his high-school football coach had also taught history class by assigning the students to answer the questions at the end of the chapter while he sat at his desk and pretended to read his history book while he dozed. And he never graded those questions after the students handed them in, either.

"What would you have done if Claude Appleby hadn't come in to get you out?" Ivy asked.

Rhodes didn't say anything because to him that wasn't the interesting question. The interesting question was, what had Claude been doing there in the first place?

"You're going to get yourself killed, one of these days," Ivy said. "You know that?"

Rhodes didn't really believe he was going to get killed, but that didn't make him unique. No one ever believed he was going to get killed, no matter how close he came. And Rhodes figured that he'd come pretty close. Like everyone else, however, he was sure the world just couldn't keep on turning without him.

"You aren't listening to me at all, are you?" Ivy said.

"I'm listening," Rhodes said.

"No you're not. You say you are, but you aren't. You don't even care if you get killed. But I care."

"I care, too," Rhodes said. "I didn't get caught in that building on purpose."

"But you get caught like that all the time."

"Not on purpose," Rhodes insisted. "It's part of the job."

"Then maybe it's time to start looking for a new job."

Rhodes smiled. Or that's what he was trying to do. In the mirror it appeared more like a pained grimace. Maybe that's what it was, because he and Ivy had had this discussion, or similar ones, more than once.

"The voters will probably tell me when it's time for a new job," he said.

"You don't have to wait for them to tell you."

"I know that, but I sort of like what I'm doing."

"You like getting blown to bits?"

Rhodes was about to point out that he was still all in one piece, but the truth was, he felt a little scattered.

"I don't like that part of it," he said. "But I do like some of it."

"Such as?"

"Such as enforcing the law."

"Someone else could do that."

"I know it. And maybe even better than I can."

Ivy looked at him in surprise.

"You know better than that. I don't ever want to hear you talk that way. You're the best sheriff in the state."

"If I'm so good, why should I quit?"

"If you don't understand," Ivy said, "then I can't explain it to you."

She stalked out of the bathroom, and Rhodes grimaced at himself in the mirror again.

The next morning Rhodes dragged himself out of bed an hour later than usual. It had been almost time to get up before he'd gotten to sleep, and he was running on a serious sleep deficit. His body was aching in places that he didn't even know could ache.

But his mind felt perfectly lucid, unlike the previous evening, when he knew he'd been thinking some pretty strange things. And when he held up two fingers, he could see them clearly.

Time to get back in the game, he thought.

"Glad to see you could make it," Hack said when Rhodes came in through the front door. "Me and Lawton were beginnin' to think we were goin' to have to run the county all by ourselves today."

"I'm sure the county would've been in good hands," Rhodes said.

Hack was sitting at his desk, and Lawton, as usual, was leaning against a wall. Rhodes tried to remember the last time he'd seen Lawton sitting down. He couldn't.

But that didn't stop Rhodes from sitting. He didn't care if Lawton never sat in a chair again.

"Bein' blowed up must not agree with you," Hack told him. "You don't look so hot, if you don't mind me sayin' so."

Rhodes settled into his chair and said he didn't mind. He knew how he looked.

"So I guess it's all right that you stayed in bed a little longer than usual, you bein' all beat up like you are," Hack said, sounding a little peeved. "Bein' in a fire and all."

"Is there some particular problem that you two have run into this morning?" Rhodes asked.

"Just the one," Hack said.

"Which one would that be?"

"You couldn't really call it a problem," Lawton said. "Not for us, that is."

Rhodes repressed a sigh and said, "Who was it a problem for, then?"

"Old Tige Barker," Hack told him.

Barker wasn't all that old, as Rhodes recalled, probably not as old as Hack. He was a retired mail carrier who lived in a well-kept little house on a shady lot just a few blocks down the street from the jail. He led a quiet life, taking care of a little garden in the spring and fall and keeping to himself most of the time. Rhodes couldn't imagine what kind of problem he might have. He knew that Hack and Lawton would tell him, though. Eventually.

"I remember when old Tige used to carry the mail on this route," Hack said. "Walked every step of it, winter and summer, rain or shine. Didn't ride in those little Jeep-lookin' carts that they run around in these days."

"Be in even more trouble if he was havin' to do that now," Lawton said.

Hack gave him a look, but it was too late. Rhodes grasped at the hint.

"Did something happen to Tige so that he can't walk? Is that it?"

Hack was still looking at Lawton, who refused to meet his eyes.

"Well?" Rhodes said.

"I guess you could say he might have a little trouble walkin'," Hack told him reluctantly.

"Why?" Rhodes asked.

"Toe problems," Hack said.

"Something's wrong with his toes?"

"Just one of 'em," Lawton said, drawing another look from Hack.

"Which one?" Rhodes asked, not sure that it mattered but certain that he wanted to stay on the subject.

"Big one," Hack said, taking control of the story before Lawton could answer.

"Left big one," Lawton added.

"What does Tige Barker's left big toe have to do with us?" Rhodes wanted to know.

"Well, it's not like he hurt it himself," Lawton said.

"Somebody else hurt it?"

"That's right," Hack said.

Rhodes felt like he was getting close to the answer now.

"Who hurt it?" he asked.

"His wife," Hack answered. "Midge."

"Hit it with a hammer," Lawton put in before Hack could.

Rhodes thought for just a second that Hack might get out of his chair and give Lawton a punch, but he didn't. He just took a deep breath and let it out slowly.

Lawton stood casually, hands in his pockets, rocking a little on his heels and admiring his friend's self-control.

"Why?" Rhodes asked.

"That's what Tige wanted you to find out," Hack said. "He wanted you to come and 'investigate the crime.' "

"What is there to investigate? We already know who did it."

"Motive," Hack said. "He wanted you to question his wife and find out the motive."

"Don't need it," Rhodes said. "In Texas, you don't have to prove motive. There are people on death row who could tell you that."

"They don't ever show that on TV," Lawton said, surprised.

"They don't have a lot of crime shows set in Texas," Hack said. "Just that one with Chuck Norris playin' a Texas Ranger."

"You ever watch that one?" Lawton asked Rhodes. "I don't think there was ever a Texas Ranger looked as scruffy as that. I think they've got a dress code or something."

"Me, too," Hack said. "They'd never hire anybody as hairy as that Chuck Norris. If you ask me—"

"Hold it," Rhodes said. "Let's get back to Tige Barker. His wife hit him with a hammer, and he wants me to find out why?"

"Not anymore," Hack said.

"Why not?"

"Because I sent Ruth Grady to investigate. She's just a deputy, so she got to work on time this mornin', not an hour or two late like the high sheriff."

"All right," Rhodes said. "I'm sorry I'm late. But I'm not required to punch a time clock. Now tell me what happened."

"Tige was eatin' breakfast. Cheerios. And he was readin' the paper. Not the Clearview paper. The Dallas paper."

"Is that why his wife hit him?"

"Depends," Hack said.

"On what?"

"On how you look at it," Lawton said.

"Wasn't because it was the Dallas paper," Hack said. "It was because all Tige ever does at breakfast is read the paper. Won't talk to Midge."

"She got tired of him sittin' there, readin' and not talkin'," Lawton said. "So she went to the toolbox and got the hammer."

"Teach Tige to go barefoot at the table," Hack said. "I think she hit that toe pretty hard. Tige says the toenail's gonna turn black and come off."

"Got old Tige's attention, though," Lawton said. "It surely did that."

"Doesn't sound like a criminal case to me," Rhodes said.

"Assault," Hack said. "That's what Tige called it. But he didn't much care if we arrested Midge or not. He just wanted to know the motive."

"Why didn't he just ask Midge?"

"He did," Lawton said. "She wouldn't tell him."

"Wouldn't talk to him at all," Hack said. "Just picked up the sports section and started starin' at it. That's what I'd call a clue if I was the sheriff."

"But Ruth got it all sorted out," Rhodes said.

"I think so. She came back here and said she had to get out to Obert and go over the crime scene again. You gonna be goin' out there, too?"

"Maybe," Rhodes said. "If there aren't any other toe emergencies for me to look into."

"I think the one was all," Hack said. "So. You goin' to Obert?"

"No," Rhodes said. "I'm going to Wal-Mart."

"Wal-Mart?" Hack said.

"Sporting goods department," Rhodes said, getting out of his chair. "If you two have any more problems you can't handle, give me a call."

21

▼

THE WAL-MART PARKING LOT WAS CROWDED, BUT NOT NEARLY as crowded as it had been when Rhodes had visited the store for the signing. He was able to get a parking spot no more than fifty yards from the door.

He went inside and walked past the clothing department, past stacks of twenty-can cartons of Dr Pepper, past stacks of twenty-five-inch TV sets, past piles of DVD players, past the jewelry department, past the displays of videos for sale, past the furniture and the dog food and the cat food and into the sporting goods department.

Claude Appleby was behind the counter, wearing a blue Wal-Mart vest with his name tag pinned to it. He was taking payment for a hunting knife when Rhodes walked up.

Rhodes passed the time until the transaction was done by looking at the display of exercise equipment, not that he was in the market for any. There were treadmills and stair-steppers and a couple of stationary bikes that made the little Huffy that Rhodes sometimes worked out on look like a child's toy.

"Thinking of getting in shape?" Claude Appleby asked at Rhodes's elbow.

"Not today," Rhodes said. "I need to talk to you, Claude."

"I'm due for my break," Claude said. "Let me make sure I got the counter covered."

Claude disappeared for a minute, then returned.

"Eddie's got it," he said. "We can go in the stockroom if you want to."

Rhodes said that would suit him just fine.

Rhodes hadn't been able to talk to Claude after the rescue because he hadn't felt like it and because they'd both had to spend time being treated by the paramedics who arrived in the ambulance. By the time that had been done, it was far too late, or too early, depending on your point of view, to do an interview. And Rhodes had been very tired, not to mention slightly addled.

The fire had not been as bad as Rhodes had feared it might be. The old fire truck was a lot more reliable than it looked, and there had been a fire hydrant not too far from the burning building after all. Clearview's trucks had come out as well, and though it had taken a while, the volunteers had gotten the fire under control.

The damage from the explosion was severe, but only to the kitchen. The other rooms were not going to be usable for a while, however, because of all the smoke and water damage.

And Rhodes wasn't too sure about the structural soundness of the building after the explosion. Chatterton was going to have to get it inspected before he could have any more conferences there, if he ever wanted to have another one after the way the first one had gone.

Rhodes had managed to do one thing after the paramedics checked him out and before he'd headed home. He'd called Ballinger, rousing him out of sleep, and told him not to release Terry Don Coslin's name to anyone until Rhodes gave him the word. Rhodes knew Ballinger couldn't hold off for long, but he also knew he wasn't going to be able to deal with the press in his current condition. He didn't like dealing with them in any condition.

Ballinger had been easy enough to persuade. He was still worried about what was going to happen when people found out that his clients were getting their fingers cut off by people who wanted to smoke them.

So Rhodes wouldn't be dealing with the press for at least another day. He was hoping he could wrap things up by then, no matter how unlikely that seemed to him now. And the first step toward doing so was going to be his interview with Claude Appleby.

There was someone standing out on the loading dock smoking a cigarette, but the stockroom was empty of people except for Rhodes and Claude. It wasn't empty of things, however. It was stacked high with cardboard boxes full of just about everything imaginable. The room smelled vaguely of Old Roy dog food, a smell with which Rhodes was intimately familiar, and there was a soft-drink machine standing next to a candy machine.

"You want a Coke?" Claude asked.

Rhodes knew that Claude didn't really mean Coca-Cola. That was just the generic word for soft drink.

"No, thanks," he said, looking at the machines.

Rhodes could remember when machines like those simply required that you put in a coin and punch a button or pull a handle to get what you wanted. Now they looked as complicated as the control panel for the Starship Enterprise.

"I want to thank you for what you did last night," Rhodes told Claude. Rhodes's sore muscles protested as the two of them settled down on a low stack of boxes. "I don't think I could've made it out of there on my own."

"I'm just glad I could help," Claude said.

"I'm glad, too," Rhodes said. "But there's something that's been bothering me."

Claude looked away from him. The man outside on the loading dock flipped his cigarette butt away and came back into the stockroom. He walked by Rhodes and Claude, said "Hey" to Claude, and disappeared into the store.

"You know what's bothering me, don't you?" Rhodes said when the man was gone.

Claude still wouldn't meet Rhodes's eye. Rhodes knew why. Claude and his twin brother had been known to wander around where they had no business being. They had a habit of looking in people's windows, and they'd occasionally even been known to pick up things that didn't belong to them, like a copy of a very rare book. Rhodes had once briefly suspected that the twins might have been involved in a murder he was investigating, but he'd finally decided that they were pretty good kids at heart and that most of their problems stemmed from their father.

But even with their father in prison, the twins, or maybe just Claude, still seemed to see more than their share of the sights around Obert. Claude was the one who'd seen the naked woman, though his mother didn't know that he had.

"I know what you're thinking, Sheriff," Claude said. "And I can't blame you. Besides, I guess you're right. I've been backslidin' a little, you might say."

"What have you been up to?" Rhodes asked.

"Nothin' much. And my brother hasn't been with me, not a single time."

"You've been doing a little prowling," Rhodes said.

"A little."

"How much is a little?"

"Like I said, nothin' much. I was walkin' around last night, and I happened to see you look out the window up in that old college building. And the next thing I knew there was that explosion. I knew you must have still been in there, and when you didn't come out, I went in after you."

"That was a brave thing to do," Rhodes said.

Claude said he hadn't thought about that.

"I just didn't want you to burn up in there."

"Me, neither," Rhodes said. "And I'm glad you didn't let me. But what I want to know is whether you saw anybody else looking out that window. Or falling out of it."

"No, sir. I saw the ambulance up there, and I guess that's what got my curiosity up. But I was watchin' TV with my mother, and she doesn't much like it when I go out of the house at night. So I had to wait till she went to bed before I could go see what was happening."

His mother had pretty good reasons for keeping an eye on her sons, Rhodes thought, but he was glad Claude had decided to leave the house anyway.

"If you were there when I looked out the window," Rhodes said, "you must've seen somebody go into the building."

"No, sir, I didn't. I was over on the same side you were on, so if anybody went in through that front door, I didn't see 'em."

"Did any lights go on downstairs?"

"There was light movin' around down there," Claude said, "but I didn't see who was holdin' it."

"What about where the explosion was?"

"All I could see was a light. And I did see somebody start a fire in there. I couldn't see who it was, though."

"How long was that before the explosion?"

"Not long. Maybe a few minutes."

That was about right, Rhodes figured. Maybe open the gas jets on the stove all the way, light a fire in a wastebasket, and get out while the getting was good.

But Rhodes still wasn't sure why it had happened.

"You didn't see anything else?" he asked.

"No, sir," Claude said. "That was it."

"You didn't see anybody fall out of that window on the third floor."

"Not me, no, sir."

Claude's voice sounded firm, but his eyes kept sliding away. Rhodes wasn't convinced that he was telling the complete truth.

"And your brother didn't see anything, either?"

"No, sir, he didn't," Claude said, looking at his wristwatch. "He's better about stayin' in the house than I am these days. My break time's about up, Sheriff. I wish I could help you out some more, but I've told you everything I know about what happened."

"All right, Claude. I appreciate your help."

Claude stood up and said, "You're not gonna arrest me, are you?"

"No," Rhodes told him. "You didn't do anything that I could arrest you for, did you?"

"No, sir. I wish you'd tell my mother that. She thinks you're gonna come arrest me any minute."

Mrs. Appleby had showed up sometime in the midst of all the excitement after the explosion, and she hadn't been happy with Claude. Rhodes hadn't heard what she said to Claude, but he could imagine that it wasn't composed entirely of commendations for his behavior.

"I'll see what I can do to relieve her mind," Rhodes said. "After all, you saved my life. But I may have to talk to you again about things."

"You know where to find me," Claude said, and headed back into the store.

22

▼

THE SPOT WHERE TERRY DON COSLIN HAD HIT THE GROUND WAS in the main building's shadow, so the light still wasn't ideal, but Rhodes saw Ruth Grady going over the spot very carefully.

"Find anything new?" he asked.

Ruth looked up and said, "I didn't expect to see you out here today."

Rhodes was reminded of how sore he was. Every muscle in his body ached, but at least his head wasn't throbbing.

"You know me," he said. "I can't resist a good crime scene."

"This isn't a very good one," Ruth said. "We should've been more careful last night."

"I thought we were careful. What's the problem?"

"Footprints."

"There weren't any."

"Well, there are now. We were here, the ambulance crew was here, the justice of the peace was here. It was like that writers' convention moved out of the building and met right where Terry Don Coslin fell."

"But everyone knows the drill. Besides, the ground's too hard to take footprints."

"The grass isn't. Look at the way it's been trampled down."

Rhodes could see the flattened blades, which would have been more easily crushed in the evening when the dew was on the ground.

"I didn't notice any of that last night," he said. "Maybe because it wasn't there."

"Maybe. But maybe the light just wasn't good. Maybe we missed something. We should've kept everyone away."

"So you think someone might have been up here and taken a look at Terry Don."

"I don't think anything, one way or the other," Ruth said. "But if someone was here, we've just about covered up all the traces of it."

Rhodes thought about the way Claude Appleby wouldn't quite look him in the eye when they were talking.

"If someone had been here, what difference would it make?" he asked.

"I don't know. But I don't like being careless."

Rhodes didn't like it, either. On the other hand, they'd done the best they could under the circumstances, and they couldn't very well have left Terry Don lying out there on the cold ground all night.

"It's possible someone came up here and looked things over after the body was moved," he said.

"Claude Appleby," Ruth said, catching on fast. "He was up here, wasn't he."

"He pulled me out of that building," Rhodes said. "I wouldn't have made it on my own. I wasn't thinking clearly at all. And I couldn't seem to stand up."

"I'm glad he pulled you out, but I wish he hadn't messed around up here."

"We don't know that he did," Rhodes reminded her.

"No, we don't, but I can't help thinking someone did. Have you talked to him today?"

Rhodes nodded. "He said he didn't do anything, but he did admit that he was standing on this side of the building."

"I knew it," Ruth said. "He's the one who messed things up. I'd bet money on it."

"Probably," Rhodes said. "And he might have seen something that he didn't mention to me. I've been wondering how whoever killed Terry Don got out of the building. Maybe he used the fire escape."

The cylindrical structure that served as a fire escape was attached to the side of the main building. If you entered it, you found that the inside was a curving slide that dumped you out on the grass. Rhodes knew because he'd been in there once before.

"Maybe he just came down the stairs," Ruth said.

"Sure. But what if he didn't want to be seen?"

"He got upstairs without being seen."

"People were still eating. Later they'd have been standing around, talking, maybe within sight of the stairs."

"Why didn't they hear Terry Don fall?"

"Because he didn't yell," Rhodes said. "And nobody was on this side of the building to hear him when he landed."

"But the killer had a look at him."

"It's possible, if he used the fire escape."

"Then what did he do?"

"He went back inside," Rhodes said. "Mingled with the crowd, and no one ever knew he'd been gone."

"Okay," Ruth said. "Let's check it out."

They looked at the exit of the fire escape, but there was no evidence that anyone had used it.

"I'll look inside," Ruth said. "Maybe there's something in there."

Rhodes agreed that checking the fire escape was a good idea.

"But we need to check the top floor again first," he said, and told her what he thought he'd seen there.

"You mean I missed something?" Ruth said.

"I'm not sure. It's probably nothing, or it might just be something that's been there for years."

"We'd better get up there and have a look, just the same."

"I'll get a flashlight," Rhodes said.

The smell of charred wood and wet carpet and smoke was almost overpowering inside the building. Water was still dripping from the ceiling.

"A least the dust won't be so bad," Rhodes said as they started up the stairs.

"Thank God for small favors," Ruth said. "Are you sure it's safe to be in here?"

"No. I'd bet it's not safe at all, if you want to know the truth. I wouldn't want any civilians coming in here, and I wouldn't be in here myself if I didn't think it was necessary."

"I'm sorry I asked," Ruth said. "You think it's going to fall down on our heads?"

"No, but there's always the possibility."

"It's a real shame. Mr. Chatterton worked hard getting this place in shape, and he must've spent a lot of money on it. It was really nice, too, something the town could be proud of. And now look at it."

Rhodes looked around at the soaked floors and the dripping walls of the second floor, trying to ignore the fact that climbing the stairs had taken quite a toll on him.

"I'm sure Chatterton feels lower than a snake's belly about the whole thing," he said. "I just hope he had good insurance."

"I wouldn't count on it," Ruth said, starting up to the third floor. "I talked to him earlier. He's crushed. If you blew on him, he'd fall over."

"What about the workshop?"

"They're going to try having their sessions in the sitting room of the dormitory. It's going to be crowded and uncomfortable, but it's the best they can do."

"Did you talk to anybody else other than Chatterton?"

"I talked to that Serena Thayer. She threw a hissy fit when I told her that she couldn't leave until the investigation was finished."

"Jeanne Arnot was upset, too," Rhodes said.

"Not as upset as Thayer, I'll bet. I thought she was going to jump me and claw my eyes out. If I hadn't been wearing a sidearm, she might've tried it."

"She would've been in for a surprise," Rhodes said.

Ruth grinned. "You got that right."

They reached the third floor without incident, though Rhodes had thought the walls might tumble down on them at any moment, no matter what he'd said to Ruth. Maybe the old building was sturdier than he'd thought.

The top floor was much drier than the other two, not that the Obert fire truck hadn't had the power to pump the water that high. It just hadn't seemed necessary. Still, it was fairly damp. The crime-scene tape was still attached to both sides of the doorway, and Rhodes pulled it off. It wasn't doing any good there.

"Where did you see something?" Ruth asked.

"It was over by the window," Rhodes said. "The light had to hit it at just the right angle."

He shined the flashlight along the cracks between the floorboards, trying to catch a glimpse of the same sparkle that he'd seen the previous night, but he couldn't locate it.

"Maybe I was just imagining things," he said after about five minutes. "I could have sworn I saw it, though."

"Exactly where were you when you saw it?" Ruth asked.

Rhodes showed her.

"But that's only a guess. Somebody moved the paint can and hit me with it."

"Evidence," Ruth said, going over to the can.

"Whoever hit me was probably holding it by the bail," Rhodes said. "There won't be any prints on that."

He touched the back of his head gingerly with his fingertips. The knot was hard and tender, and he wished he hadn't touched it.

"There might be some of my hair on that can," he said. "But I don't think that'll be much help to us."

Ruth didn't think so, either. She left the can sitting where it was.

"Just try to get as close to where you were as you can," she said. "Maybe you'll find it this time."

Rhodes tried again, but it was no use. There was not the faintest glimmer of a reflection in the flashlight's beam.

"I think somebody came up here and found it," Ruth said. "That's why you got conked."

"Could be," Rhodes said. "Or the explosion could have shaken the thing deeper into one of the cracks. But whatever it was, it's not here now."

Ruth didn't want to give up the search.

"It could still be here and we missed it. We need to keep looking."

"I don't think so," Rhodes said. "I have a feeling it's gone. But if it's still here, and if we need it, we can always come back for it."

"All right," Ruth said, giving in reluctantly. "What are we going to do next?"

"You can check the fire escape first. Then go back to town to see what's going on around the county. Hack and Lawton are likely to panic at the responsibility."

"They told you about Tige Barker," Ruth said.

"They did. And you never know when another emergency will come up."

"I'll try not to panic if it does," Ruth said. "But just in case I do, where will you be?"

"Talking to the writers."

"Don't let that Serena jump you. I don't trust her."

Ruth's eyes narrowed when she mentioned Serena's name, and Rhodes wondered if maybe Ruth suspected Serena of having killed Terry Don.

"You don't like her much, do you," he said.

"Not even a little bit. She's way too high-strung to suit me."

Rhodes had to agree, but he felt he had to mention that being high-strung wasn't a crime in Texas. "And," he added, "I don't think I'll be talking to her yet, anyway."

"Who're you going to talk to then?"

"Belinda Marshall," Rhodes said.

"Did she know Terry Don?"

"I think so," Rhodes told her. "From what I hear, everybody knew Terry Don. One way or another."

"Oh," Ruth said.

23

▼

RHODES MANAGED TO PERSUADE BELINDA MARSHALL THAT IT was more important that she talk to him than attend a workshop session on "The Arc of the Story."

"I don't really mind missing it," Belinda said. "After all, it's only Marian. I've heard her talk before, and it's not like she'll come up with anything new."

Rhodes was a little surprised. He told Belinda that he'd always thought writers came up with new things to say all the time.

Belinda laughed. "That might be true when they're writing, but not when they're talking. Most of them are like tape recorders. When you give them a topic, it's like punching the play button. You get the same thing every time."

Rhodes and Belinda were sitting outside the dormitory in plastic lawn chairs beside a plastic table under a tall pecan tree. They'd had to brush the leaves out of the chairs before they could sit. The chairs and table had once been white, but they'd been outside for a while and they hadn't been cleaned often. If ever. There were dark spots of something that Rhodes suspected might be mildew on them here and there.

Belinda rummaged around in her leather Dooney and Bourke bag and came out with a Marlboro hard pack and a butane lighter.

"You don't mind if I smoke, do you?"

Rhodes said he didn't mind, and Belinda looked on the table for an ashtray. There wasn't one.

"I'll just use the yard," she said. "I don't think anyone will mind, do you?"

Rhodes said he didn't think so.

Belinda lit her Marlboro, took a deep drag, and tossed her head, shaking the long braid that hung down her back.

"I was looking at some book covers yesterday," Rhodes said. "I saw one of yours."

"Which one?" she asked, exhaling smoke.

"I think it was called something like *Passion in the Pines*."

Belinda laughed again. "Sounds good, but it's not one of mine. Try again."

"Was I close?"

"Not really. I do have one coming out in a month or two called *The Passionate Pirate*."

"That's the one," Rhodes said. "The pirate looked a lot like Terry Don Coslin."

"I had a feeling we'd get around to talking about him sooner or later," Belinda said, flipping ashes on the grass.

"He did have quite a reputation," Rhodes said. "If you know what I mean."

"I know, all right. Everybody knows. It's not as if it's a secret. And I already know what your next question is."

Rhodes wondered if she'd save him the trouble of asking it, and she did.

"I never slept with him," she said. "I didn't have to. I'm not big enough to have any influence on the cover selection for my books. It was just the luck of the draw. But if I'd had a choice,

I'd have asked for Terry D. on my cover anyway. He didn't have to sleep with me. His picture was worth a lot in sales. I think *The Passionate Pirate* would have sold an extra ten thousand copies because of it."

"Would have?" Rhodes said.

"Now that he's dead, it'll probably sell an extra twenty-five thousand copies. Maybe more."

"So dying was a good career move."

"I've heard that one before. But it wasn't so good for Terry D. For me, maybe."

"You realize that you're giving yourself a pretty good motive for murder, I guess," Rhodes said.

Belinda flicked some more ashes into the air and watched them settle to the grass.

"Let me tell you something, Sheriff," she said. "You might think I'm like some of those other women in there, but I'm not. It's true that most of them would kill to sell a few more books, but I wouldn't. I don't need the fame, and I certanly don't need the money."

"I thought everybody could use a little money," Rhodes said.

"Not everybody's a millionaire," Belinda said.

She dropped her cigarette to the ground and crushed it with the toe of her shoe.

"You've made a million dollars as a writer?" Rhodes said.

"Of course not," Belinda told him. "Nobody does that, at least not anybody I know. Nora Roberts does, and Sandra Brown does, but I don't know them. You don't run into them at workshops like this one for some reason. Anyway, I made my money in the stock market."

"You play the stock market?"

Rhodes was surprised. He thought writers sat around in their studies, surrounded by books, and wrote all the time.

"I don't *play*," Belinda said. "I work at it. I do research. I study trends. I bought Dell Computer when it went public. I bought Amazon.com early on. I bought Qualcomm when it was under fifty dollars a share."

Rhodes didn't know much about the stock market, but he did know about Dell Computer, because it was a Texas firm. And he'd heard about the amazing success of Amazon.com.

"If you have so much money, why do you write?" he asked.

"That's what writers do," Belinda said. "It's not as if we have a choice. Making money is just a sideline."

Rhodes thought about his conversation with Ivy. He couldn't explain to her why he continued in his job, but if he'd thought of it, and if he'd had a way with words, he might have put it just the way Belinda had. Ivy thought he had a choice. He wasn't so sure that was true.

"Are we finished?" Belinda asked. "I might want to attend the next session."

"I guess we're finished, for now," Rhodes said. "Marian Willoughby's not doing the next session, is she?"

"No. Serena is. Why?"

"Because Marian is the one I want to talk to."

"Why her?"

"Because she's the one who didn't seem to remember where you were when Henrietta was killed," Rhodes said.

Belinda sat back in her chair and considered Rhodes. Then she got out another cigarette, lit it, exhaled, and said, "You bastard."

"Sneaky, maybe," Rhodes said. "But that's about the extent of it."

"I didn't think you even noticed that little bit with Marian," Belinda said.

"And observant," Rhodes said. "Sneaky and observant."

"And a bastard."

"If you say so."

"You think I killed Henrietta and Terry Don both, don't you."

"I don't know what to think. I'm still trying to sort things out and let the pieces fall into place."

Rhodes wasn't lying. He thought he knew some of what had happened, or at least he was constructing a scenario that would explain a lot of things, but he hadn't reached any conclusions so far.

"Well, I didn't kill either one of them," Belinda said. "I'm not even in Henrietta's stupid little book."

"So you've heard about that," Rhodes said.

"Everybody's heard about it. The ones who didn't know before she was killed know now. It's the talk of the workshop."

Rhodes should have known.

"You might not be in the book, but you weren't with Marian Willoughby when Henrietta died," he said. "Were you?"

"No. If you must know, I wasn't. I'd sneaked off for a smoke, and I thought it might look bad for me if I said I was off by myself. So I asked Marian to say I was with her."

"Why did you think you'd need an alibi?"

"I didn't think that. I just didn't want any trouble."

"So you really don't have anyone to vouch for you," Rhodes said.

"No. But when you think about it, neither does Marian. And I can think of a few questions you could ask that woman with the funny red hair, by the way, when you get through worrying about me."

"Lorene?"

"I think that's her name. Where does she buy her hair coloring?"

Rhodes said he didn't have any idea.

"What should I ask her?" he said.

"You could ask her where she was when Henrietta died. She was Henrietta's roomie, after all."

"I know, but she doesn't have a motive. And she was with two other women when Henrietta died."

"That's what she told you. I heard her. But is it the truth?"

"Is there any reason to think they'd lie for her?"

"Maybe not," Belinda said, blowing out a smoky plume. "But Marian lied for me."

"Not very well," Rhodes pointed out.

"True. But it's something to think about."

"I've already thought about it. I'm going to check on everyone's alibis."

"What if they're all fabricated, like mine was?"

"Then I'll have an even longer list of suspects," Rhodes said.

"I suppose I'm still on the list, then."

"As a matter of fact," Rhodes said, "you are."

"What would I have to do to get off?"

"Prove you're not guilty."

"I'm not sure I can do that. But if I were the sheriff, I know I'd find out about that redhead. Lorene. What's with the names of people around here, anyway? Lorene. Vernell. Henrietta."

"Don't forget Belinda," Rhodes said.

Belinda laughed. "You've got me there. I guess not everyone can be named Jennifer or Tracy."

"Right."

"But no matter what my name is, I didn't kill anyone. I promise."

"I'll keep that in mind," Rhodes said.

24
▼

THE PERSON RHODES WANTED TO TALK TO NOW WASN'T MARIAN or Lorene. It was Chatterton. Rhodes went back to the dormitory with Belinda and located Chatterton sitting in the front room, alone.

"The session's about over," he told Rhodes listlessly. "Everyone's in there except me. I wasn't interested."

Rhodes asked him to come outside and have a talk.

"It's a nice day," Rhodes said. "The sunshine will do you good."

Chatterton didn't seem to think so, but he went along.

"How are you going to handle lunch today?" Rhodes asked.

"Somebody from the Round-Up will be bringing it out in a little while," Chatterton said. "They'll set up some tables out here, and we'll eat under the pecan trees. I guess I should be thankful that it isn't raining."

"It's too bad about the building," Rhodes said.

Chatterton stood looking out over the countryside and didn't say anything for a while. Then he looked over at the main building. The outside stones in the kitchen area were black from the smoke and fire damage.

When Chatterton finally spoke, there was a catch in his voice.

"It's not just the building," he said. "I can't believe everything that's happened here. Two people have been killed, and everything I worked for is ruined."

"You must've had insurance," Rhodes said.

Chatterton walked over to one of the plastic chairs and sat down. His shoulders slumped, and he looked utterly defeated.

"Not enough, if you're thinking I'm the one who tried to burn it," he said. "I would never have done that, not for any amount of money. I worked for two years to make this place what it is, and now it's all wasted."

"The building can be repaired," Rhodes said.

"Not easily. Those old buildings are a lot more fragile than they look. It would take a lot of time and money, and I'm not sure I'm up to going through all that again. Do you know why I did it in the first place?"

"To make money?" Rhodes guessed.

"Absolutely not. I hoped to get back my investment eventually, sure, but that's not why I did it. I told you about my name, didn't I?"

"You said something about not being related to an English poet, but that's all."

"Thomas Chatterton. My parents were university English professors, and with the family name being what it was, they couldn't resist naming me Thomas."

"I don't remember him from school," Rhodes said.

"There's no reason why you should. He was a very minor poet, and he died before he was eighteen. But he produced some remarkable work in his short life. I never produced anything, which was a big disappointment to my parents."

"You were a poet?"

"No. I tried. And I tried fiction and nonfiction, too. But nothing I wrote was ever published. Luckily I had a real job, like most of those people in there. When my parents died, they left me a little money, and I thought about using it to help writers. I'd heard about this place and what Simon Graham tried to do with it. I knew it was vacant and for sale, so I decided it would be my contribution to literature. Now it doesn't look that way at all."

"But you have the money to rebuild, don't you?"

"No. And the insurance won't help. I was underinsured, if anything. Who would ever have thought something like that would happen?"

No one, Rhodes thought. It took a unique combination of people and events to bring it all about. But there was a chance that Chatterton had been a part of it.

"You told me the other night that you were in the dormitory when Henrietta was killed," Rhodes said. "You were checking to make sure everything was in order and the people had everything they needed. I didn't hear anybody back you up on that."

Chatterton opened his mouth, then closed it.

"I thought you were interested in my insurance," he said after a few seconds.

"I was," Rhodes said. "For a while. Now I'm interested in something else."

"Why can't we just stick to one subject?"

Rhodes didn't have an answer for that one. His interview technique wasn't anything he'd learned in a class or from a book. It was just something that had developed over the years. He wasn't sure that jumping from one topic to another gave any better results than anything else, but it was something he did from time to time. It certainly seemed to have disconcerted Chatterton.

"I didn't kill anyone," Chatterton said.

"But you weren't in the dormitory."

"No," Chatterton said. "I wish I had been, but I wasn't."

"You were watching television," Rhodes said.

"How in the world did you know that?"

"I guessed. I saw the TV set in your room, and I remembered what you said about there not being any television here because you believed in reading and writing, not watching TV."

"I did say that, didn't I?"

"But you didn't mean it, at least not for yourself."

Chatterton sighed. "I suppose not. I wish I did, but ever since I gave up writing, I find that I don't like reading very much. It makes me feel inferior somehow to read a book by someone who really can't write any better than I can, or at least it seems to me they can't, and to know that they've sold not only that book but others besides. And that they're widely read and popular."

"In other words," Rhodes said, "you're jealous."

"I don't like the word, but I suppose it fits."

Rhodes made a leap of faith, or maybe it was just another guess.

"You weren't jealous of Henrietta, though. You were jealous of Vernell."

Chatterton looked beyond surprise.

"How on earth did you know that?"

Rhodes could have said it was just a hunch, but he didn't want to reveal trade secrets. Besides, there was more to it than that.

"Because she wasn't anybody. Just some woman from a small town in the middle of Texas. She keeps goats in her yard. And yet she'd sold a book, and you hadn't."

Chatterton grimaced and said, "You're right, sort of. I'm not so much jealous as I am envious. And it gets worse."

"How?"

"She's got the best agent in the business for her next book."

"She has?"

"It's the latest hot gossip. Even better than Terry Don Coslin's death and Henrietta's manuscript. Jeanne Arnot is going to take

Vernell as a client. She thinks she can get six figures for her next book."

Rhodes had liked *Wild Texas Wind,* but he hadn't thought it was *that* good. Well, he was no judge of literature. Maybe he was just envious, like Chatterton.

"Good for Vernell," he said, to prove he wasn't.

"If you think I'm envious," Chatterton said, "you should talk to some of those other prepublished writers."

"Prepublished?"

"Okay, *un*published, then."

"I'd think they'd be happy for Vernell."

"Oh, they are. In a way. But they all wish it could have been them."

Rhodes couldn't blame them. Six figures. It had a nice sound. But Chatterton was as good as Hack and Lawton at getting off the subject. Rhodes got back to it.

"About that TV set," he said. "What were you watching?"

"That millionaire show," Chatterton said.

"There are a lot of those these days," Rhodes said.

"The original one. *Who Wants to Be a Millionaire.* I like to watch it because it makes me feel superior to the people on it, at least for a little while."

"You feel superior? How?"

"The questions are so easy and silly that anyone could answer them."

"I can't," Rhodes said, not feeling superior. "Not always."

"It's not a matter of knowledge, at least of important things. The questions don't test that. They're nothing but trivia."

"I see what you mean," Rhodes said.

"I thought you would. But I don't want the writers I invite here to know that I'm sneaking off to watch a show like that. Or any other show. So I kept it quiet."

"And you don't let them have TV sets in their rooms."

"No. It's a gimmick, okay? I admit it. But I didn't kill anyone because they found out I was watching television."

"I didn't think so," Rhodes said. "But Terry Don knew, didn't he."

"He knew, but he didn't care. After all, he was reading a mystery novel. I don't think he wanted anybody here to know that, either. He wanted them all to think he was reading their historical romance novels. It was like a joke between us."

"That show was over a long time before Henrietta was killed, though," Rhodes said. "You might've watched it after dinner, but it didn't last until nearly eleven-thirty."

Chatterton looked sheepish. He said, "There are a few other shows I watch now and then. One of them is the ten o'clock news."

"And after that?"

"Letterman," Chatterton said. "I know he's juvenile, but I can't help it. I sort of enjoy it."

"So do the Applebys," Rhodes said.

"Who are they?"

"They live near here," Rhodes said.

"I haven't met them. Anyway, that's what I was watching. When the musical guest came on, I left. I hardly ever care for the musical guest."

"And that's when the screaming started?"

"It started before I got there," Chatterton said. "I may have implied something else."

"You may have, all right."

"I'm sorry. But now you know the whole story." Chatterton glanced back toward the dormitory. "Can I go now? I have to get things ready for lunch."

"Go ahead," Rhodes said, and Chatterton got up and walked away.

Rhodes felt sorry for Chatterton, in a way. For most of his life the man had apparently been trying to live up to the name of some doomed British poet, and he'd never succeeded. Then he'd finally accomplished something to be proud of, and it had been virtually destroyed, all in one weekend.

But somehow Rhodes couldn't rid himself of the nagging notion that Chatterton might have had a hand in his own destruction.

25

▼

RHODES WAS STILL SITTING UNDER THE PECAN TREE WHEN A
van drove up. The words *The Round-Up* were painted on the
side in letters that appeared to be made of rope. There was a
picture of a very large steer under the name, and the restaurant's
motto was printed under the steer in black letters: ABSOLUTELY
NO CHICKEN, FISH, OR VEGETARIAN DISHES CAN BE FOUND ON
OUR MENU! Rhodes figured it must be quite an aggravation for
the owner, Sam Blevins, to provide vegetarian dishes for Serena
Thayer, but he supposed there were times a man had to go
against his beliefs in order to satisfy his customers. If anyone
mentioned it, Blevins could always say the dishes were "off the
menu."

Blevins pulled his gray Suburban to a stop behind the van and
got out. He was around six feet tall and wire thin, and Rhodes
thought he looked like a walking advertisement for a high-
protein diet. He was dressed in his usual outfit: a white western
shirt, starched and ironed Wranglers, and low-heeled black boots.

Rhodes sat and watched as Blevins directed the unloading of

the van. Before long, several long tables had been set up under the trees near the dormitory and folding chairs had been placed around them.

Rhodes wondered what the main course of the lunch would be. And he wondered if there might be an extra plate for a hungry law officer who was willing to pay his way. He strolled over to where Blevins was directing the placement of folding chairs and said hello.

"Hey, Sheriff," Blevins said. "What happened to you? You look like you wrestled a bear and lost. Or maybe tied."

"It wasn't a bear," Rhodes said. "It was a building."

Blevins looked over at the smoke- and water-stained exterior of the main building and said, "I take it back. Looks like you won."

"I don't think anybody won. What's for lunch?"

Blevins said that the menu for the day was barbecued brisket, pinto beans, coleslaw, and potato salad.

"With jalapeño peppers, onions, and pickles if you want 'em. Iced tea to drink. And then there's cherry cobbler with vanilla ice cream for dessert."

"Are you sure it's safe to serve potato salad?"

"Don't worry. It's been kept cold all the way here, and we'll be serving it right out of the containers. You won't have anybody dying of ptomaine."

"That's good to know. But I didn't think you served vegetable dishes."

Blevins made a face. "I wish you hadn't mentioned that. But they go with the meat, and they'll help with the special vegetable plate, which, God help me, is steamed carrots, cauliflower, and broccoli. Can you believe it? Who'd eat that kind of stuff?"

"Vegetarians," Rhodes said.

Blevins rolled his eyes. "What planet do those people come from?"

"This one, I think," Rhodes said.

"Well, I sure as hell don't understand 'em, and that's all I have to say about that."

"Any chance that you could set an extra plate?" Rhodes said.

Blevins stared at him in mock horror.

"Of the brisket, I mean. Not the vegetables. I'll pay."

"Heck, Sheriff, after what you did, solvin' that moose-head murder at my place, you can eat for free any time you want to."

"I believe in paying my way. How much?"

Blevins didn't haggle. "Six seventy-five."

Rhodes got seven dollars from his billfold. That left him with twenty dollars in case he found something else to spend it on.

"I don't have any change," Blevins said when Rhodes handed him the money.

"The quarter's the tip."

Blevins grinned. "That's about right."

He went over to the van and helped unload the big pans of food and set them up on the tables over the cans of Sterno that would keep them warm.

Just as everything was finished, people started filing out of the dormitory. Rhodes spotted Claudia and Jan and went to ask if he could join them for lunch.

"Sure," Claudia said. "We could probably use the protection, considering what's been going on around here. But you don't look up to putting up much of a fight if it came to that."

"He might surprise you," Jan said. "He looks pretty tough to me."

"I'm not tough," Rhodes said. "Just sore. Let's get in line."

They were served on paper plates and handed a sealed plastic bag that held plastic eating utensils, a paper napkin, and two small packets of salt and pepper. It wasn't easy to eat barbecue on a paper plate, not if you put enough sauce on it. But Rhodes was willing to make the effort.

After they were served, they found seats at the end of one of the tables where they had an excellent view of a large part of Blacklin County. The sky was clear and blue for the most part, and they could see for miles, but there was a heavy, dark blue cloud in the north that meant a change in the weather was heading their way.

Rhodes wasn't interested in the view or the weather, however. He was more interested in the people seated next to them and at the nearby tables. Lorene Winslow was at another table talking to a woman Rhodes didn't know. Vernell Lindsey was sitting by Jeanne Arnot. The two of them had their heads together, and they were engaged in an intense conversation. Rhodes wondered if they were discussing the market price of Vernell's new book.

Chatterton was sitting alone at the end of the table. It wasn't as if people were avoiding him, Rhodes thought. He just didn't seem interested in having any company.

Belinda Marshall, Marian Willoughby, and Serena Thayer were together, chatting amiably. Rhodes wondered if they really got along well or if they were sticking together because they were the real professionals in the group.

"This is a beautiful place," Jan said. She took a drink of tea from a plastic glass and then set it back on the table. "It's too bad such terrible things have been happening."

Claudia looked at Rhodes speculatively.

"And speaking of terrible things," she said, "I'll bet you didn't ask to sit with us just because we're from out of town and looked lonely. Or am I wrong?"

"You're not wrong," Rhodes admitted after taking a bite of the barbecue, which was fork-tender and delicious. "Where are you from, by the way?"

"I'm from Dallas," Claudia said. "My husband works for the county, and I'm a social worker. I've known Jan for years. She's from a little town to the east of Dallas, and she and her husband both work at a college there. She's a dean. Do you think she looks like a dean?"

Rhodes said he wasn't sure what a dean was supposed to look like.

"They're supposed to be gnarly old men," Jan said.

Claudia nodded. "And she's not a bit gnarly. Anyway, we heard about this workshop, and we knew we had to come."

"Why?" Rhodes asked.

"Because we're trying to sell a historical romance that we collaborated on," Claudia said.

"And because Jeanne Arnot was going to be here," Jan said. "She's the best agent there is. There was an article about her in *Romantic Times* not long ago. Serena Thayer's one of the best writers in the business, too. We knew we could learn a lot from the two of them."

"Like all about the arc of the story," Rhodes said, recalling the session he'd asked Belinda Marshall to skip.

"Right! But we didn't think we'd get involved in two murders and an explosion," Claudia said.

"That's a bonus, all right," Jan said. "We may be able to use it all in a book."

"You're going to write a mystery novel next, I guess," Rhodes said.

"We both think it would be a good idea," Claudia said. "You know, we've been talking about our plot, and we might be able to help you solve the murders."

Rhodes ate some more barbecue and some pinto beans. He tried the potato salad and the coleslaw. Everything was good, though he thought there was too much salad dressing in the potato salad and the slaw.

"All right," he said after a while, resigning himself. "Tell me your plot."

"The way we see it," Jan said, "is that one of the writers did it. She's sure she'll get away with it because there's no connection between her and the people she killed."

That was an interesting idea. Here Rhodes had been spending

all his time in the naïve belief that the murderer knew her (or his; Rhodes wasn't letting Chatterton off the hook) victims, when he should have been considering the fact that somebody might be going around killing strangers.

"Why would she kill people she didn't know?" he asked.

"Not that she didn't know," Claudia said. "She might know them slightly, but she wouldn't have any connection with them. Or not much of one."

"Okay," Rhodes said. "But why kill them?"

"It's obvious," Jan said. "To get a plot for her book."

"You mean she'd write about a workshop like this one where someone was killing people she didn't know so she'd have a plot for a mystery novel?"

"That's right, more or less."

"But wouldn't the book be a dead giveaway when it was published?"

"Of course not," Claudia said. "She wouldn't set the book at a workshop. She'd set it at a glamorous vacation resort or a fashionable dude ranch. Or maybe at some spectacular festival, like Mardi Gras in New Orleans. Or maybe the Battle of the Flowers parade in San Antonio."

"And she wouldn't have a sheriff as the detective," Jan said. "No offense."

"None taken," Rhodes said. "Who would she have doing the detecting?"

"A feisty female TV news reporter," Claudia said. "Whose husband has recently died tragically of some terrible disease, leaving her with beautiful sad eyes and an air of mystery."

The thought of feisty TV news reporters momentarily spoiled Rhodes's appetite. He was dreading facing them. But if he could get everything taken care of, he wouldn't have to. Or if he did, he wouldn't have to face them for long.

"And the murders would have to be a lot more gruesome," Jan said. "There wasn't enough blood in these two."

"Probably someone would have to die in the explosion, too," Claudia said thoughtfully. "Or maybe just be tragically maimed for life."

"The TV reporter's cameraman!" Jan said.

"Great idea!"

Claudia got a Mont Blanc ballpoint and a small leather notebook from her purse. She flipped the notebook open and started writing in it. When she was done, she flipped the notebook closed and stuck it back in the purse with the pen.

"What do you think, Sheriff?" she said. "Are we on the right track?"

While they had been discussing the plot of the book, the dark cloud had been moving steadily closer. Now the wind was beginning to pick up out of the north. It was cool, and there was the smell of rain in it. Several people were looking in that direction and Lorene Wilson pointed to a flicker of lightning in the cloud.

"Who knows?" Rhodes said about the plot idea. "You two could have it all figured out. I think I'll have some of that cobbler and ice cream. Can I get some for either of you?"

The two women still hadn't finished their barbecue, so Rhodes got the cobbler and ice cream for himself. It was served in a paper bowl.

When he was seated at the table again, he said, "I'd like to ask you two something, if you don't mind."

"We knew you'd get around to it sooner or later," Jan said. "Are we suspects?"

"Not at all," Rhodes said. "Unless you've been killing people you don't have any connection with so you'll have a plot for your novel."

"You're making fun of us, aren't you,?" Claudia said.

"No. I just have to follow up on my own theory, though, in case I'm right and you're not."

"Okay. I can see that, and besides, I've never been grilled before. It might be fun. Go ahead."

"I don't think this really counts as grilling. Lorene Winslow says that she was talking to the two of you when Henrietta was killed. Is that the truth?"

"I hope you don't think we'd tell a lie," Claudia said.

"Unless it was going to help us get away with killing people we're not connected with," Jan said. "In that case, you'd have to expect a lie or two."

"But we're not lying about Lorene," Claudia said. "She's a very nice woman, and we were just giving her a little advice about hair coloring."

Both she and Jan looked over to the other table, and considered Lorene. The wind was blowing a bit harder now, and Lorene's hair was moving with it. She patted it back into place with her hand, seemingly unaware that she was being watched and talked about.

"That shade of red she uses is all wrong for her," Jan said. "I think she should go with something a little more brunette."

"But anyway," Claudia said, "we were with her all the time. She's innocent."

Rhodes had thought that was the case. As far as he knew, Lorene had no reason to kill Henrietta. The character of Lorraine in Henrietta's manuscript had come off pretty well compared to most of the others, and there was nothing else between the two women as far as Rhodes knew.

"I'm glad to hear that," he said. "And of course that means the two of you are in the clear."

"I thought you'd already said we weren't suspects," Jan reminded him.

"Only if you weren't killing strangers to get a plot," Rhodes said. "In that case, I'd have to take you in, lock you up, and throw away the key."

"I think there are a couple of people at the college who might pay you to do that," Jan said. "Do you take bribes?"

"You should know better than that," Claudia told her. "You can tell by looking that he's an honest man."

Rhodes didn't think he looked honest. He thought he looked beaten up and maybe a little bit overweight, but not particularly honest. And if he looked honest, that wouldn't mean that he actually was. An honest man probably wouldn't be eating cobbler and ice cream while planning not to mention his indulgence to his wife later on.

The cloud was moving faster than ever, casting a black shadow over the fields less than a mile away. The lightning was flickering in and out of the cloud, from which a hard rain had begun to fall.

Sam Blevins came out of the van and asked everyone to take the paper plates, the disposable utensils, and any other trash and put it all in two large plastic trash cans that had been placed by the van.

"And hustle it up," Blevins said. "Before we all get wet."

Rhodes looked at the rain moving toward them and decided he'd leave the last bite of cobbler in the bowl.

26

▼

RHODES WASN'T IN A GOOD MOOD AS HE DROVE THE COUNTY
car back toward Clearview. He hadn't wanted to leave Obert
before talking to several other people, but when he checked with
Hack, the dispatcher had said that there was another emergency.

"The ghost is back," he said.

"There was never a ghost in the first place," Rhodes said.
"And if there was, I got rid of it."

"Yeah, well, that's your story. I wouldn't try tellin' that to the
prisoners."

Rhodes was having trouble hearing Hack because the rain was
pounding very hard on the roof of the county car, producing a
kind of continuous roar.

"Can't Ruth handle things?" he asked.

"She's got her own emergency. Soon as the rain started, an
eighteen-wheeler skidded off the road out near the Wal-Mart and
wound up in the bar ditch. It's a mess out there."

Rhodes could imagine. About the only way to create a traffic
jam in Blacklin County, aside from a celebrity book-signing
event, was to have an accident near Wal-Mart, which was where

172

all the traffic was. And the rain would just make everything
worse.

"Anybody hurt?" he asked.

"Not that I heard of."

"That's good. If Ruth is investigating, who's directing the traffic on the highway?"

"Buddy's doing it."

"All right. I guess that's covered. Where's the ghost?"

"At Ballinger's funeral home. Some guy drove past there and
saw it. Called it in on a cell phone."

"How does he know it was a ghost?"

"Says it must be. Weird lights flashin' on and off all over the
place."

"Did you call Ballinger?"

"First thing. Both places, his office and the funeral home.
Didn't get an answer at the office, and I got the answering machine at the funeral home. Maybe the ghost's got him." Hack
paused, then said, "Not that anybody seems to care, but I'd care
if I was the sheriff. You never can tell what those lights might
be. If it's not a ghost, it might be somebody tryin' to smoke a
finger. Or maybe they went for a big toe this time."

"I'll be there in ten minutes," Rhodes said.

It took him a little longer than that because of the rain, but he
got there as quickly as he could with the water sluicing across
his windshield and causing his car to hydroplane unnervingly
when it hit the puddles where the rain was blowing and washing
over the road. The high wind shook the car, lightning crackled,
and thunder crashed. If ever there was a time for a ghost to come
back, this was it.

Except, as Rhodes had pointed out to Hack, there had never
been a ghost in the first place, no matter what the prisoners
thought.

All the houses in the neighborhood around the funeral home were dark. There were no streetlights, either, and the whole area was murky as midnight, though it was only around one-thirty in the afternoon. Probably lightning had struck a transformer, Rhodes thought.

The funeral home itself wasn't exactly dark. Rhodes could see a faint whitish light in some of the windows, which meant that Ballinger was prepared for emergencies, as Rhodes would have expected. There was also a light in the little building that Ballinger used for an office.

When Rhodes parked the county car in back of the funeral home, he saw a flash of bright light on the inside. A few seconds passed, and then there was another flash. It didn't look much like a ghost to Rhodes, but he couldn't figure out what it was. There was no reason for a fluorescent lamp, a candle, or an old-fashioned coal-oil lamp to flash like that.

Rhodes got out of the car and ran for the back door of the funeral home, getting thoroughly wet and cold before he was able to get under cover again.

When he was inside, he stood there dripping water, watching for the flash. It came again, and then again. Rhodes walked down a hall, the rubber soles of his shoes squeaking on the polished hardwood floor, and went into one of the rooms where viewings were held.

There was a battery-powered fluorescent lamp sitting on a table in one corner. An open casket stood to one side. Rhodes saw the body of an old man he didn't recognize in the casket.

A heavyset younger man stood near the casket, holding a camera. He either hadn't heard Rhodes enter the room or didn't care that he was there. He was muttering to himself and taking pictures of the dead man.

Rhodes cleared his throat loudly, and the man turned around.

"Sorry to bother you," Rhodes said. "What's going on?"

The man held up the camera and said, "I'm taking pictures, that's what."

"I can see that," Rhodes said. "But why?"

"Why? You want to know why?"

"That's right," Rhodes said. "I do."

"Because my mother made me, that's why."

The man was younger than the one in the casket, but he was no kid. Rhodes guessed that he was in his late forties.

"Your mother made you?" Rhodes said.

"That's right. I told her I didn't want to, but she wouldn't let me off that easy. She put the old guilt trip on me. She said Aunt Ellie was too old to do it herself. That's Aunt Ellie's husband in the casket there. Uncle Roger. Who was too cheap to buy Aunt Ellie a camera, even if she were able to take pictures herself, which she isn't. So here I am."

"Taking pictures," Rhodes said.

"Anything wrong with that?"

"I guess not."

"There must not be. You should see our family albums. Half of 'em are filled with pictures of people in caskets. There's a picture of Uncle Earl in one of 'em. He was Aunt Ellie's big brother. Every time Mama sees that picture, she says, 'That's the only picture we have of Earl.' Me, I'd just as soon have no picture at all. How about you?"

Rhodes said he wasn't fond of pictures of dead people.

"Well, my family sure is. And you want to know what makes it worse?"

Rhodes wasn't sure he did, but he said, "What?"

"I have to go out after the funeral tomorrow and take pictures of the grave, that's what. It's not enough that our family albums are full of pictures of people in caskets. We gotta have pictures of their graves, too. And you want to guess what else?"

Rhodes said he didn't think so.

"That's all right. I don't blame you. You couldn't guess it if

I gave you ten years. So I'll just tell you. I have to go back when the headstone's put in, and I have to get pictures of that, too. We could have a whole book devoted to just the headstones if we wanted to separate 'em out."

The man paused and looked at Rhodes. It finally seemed to dawn on him who he was talking to.

"You're the sheriff, right?"

Rhodes agreed that he was.

"You here to arrest me? Because I don't think there's any law against what I'm doing. God knows, I wish there was. Anyway, Mr. Ballinger knows I'm in here. He's had to deal with my crazy family before."

"I'm not here to arrest you," Rhodes said. "It's just that somebody reported some strange lights here, and we've had some other problems lately. So I had to check it out."

"I didn't mean to bother anybody," the man said. "I'd have been gone before now if the lights hadn't gone out. It's not easy to be sure you have a good shot when you're working half in the dark. But I'm about done. Just four or five more shots, and I'll have both rolls finished."

"Two rolls?" Rhodes said.

"Hard to believe, right? But Mama always wants two rolls. Twenty-four shots on a roll. No more, no less. One thing about working in the dark, though, the pictures are gonna be pretty darn spooky. I don't know if that's a good thing or not. I guess Mama'll have to decide."

"Just for the record," Rhodes said, "I'll need your name and address."

"Gil Blanton," the man said, and gave Rhodes his address. "But, like I said, Mr. Ballinger knows I'm here. You can ask him."

"Don't worry," Rhodes said. "I will."

27
▼

BALLINGER WAS SITTING AT HIS DESK, HOVERING OVER A NOTE-book computer, concentrating on the screen. There was a fluorescent lantern on a table, but the light from the screen was what illuminated the funeral director's face.

"Thank God for battery-powered computers," Ballinger said, looking up. "There are five more minutes left in this auction, and I'd have missed out completely if I'd been hooked up to electricity."

"What if the battery plays out?" Rhodes asked.

"Don't even mention that. Besides, I have an hour left on this one at least. And I have a spare."

"How about the telephone line?"

"What about it?"

"Don't you have to be hooked into it?"

"I am."

"So that's why Hack couldn't get you," Rhodes said. "You should have a separate line for that computer. How are people supposed to get in touch with you?"

"They can call the other building," Ballinger said. "There's an answering machine there."

"What if it's an emergency?"

"Like what?"

"Like a ghost."

"There's no such thing as ghosts. If there were, I'm pretty sure I'd have seen one by now, considering the kind of business I'm in. And I haven't seen a single one."

"Not everybody's in your kind of business. Funny lights scare some people."

"Gil Blanton," Ballinger said, figuring out what Rhodes was talking about. "I never thought about him scaring anybody, being so used to him. I guess somebody put in a call."

"That's right," Rhodes said. "And—"

Ballinger held up a hand for silence. He was staring at the screen again.

"Not now," he said. "I have to make this final bid."

He tapped the keys of the notebook as the light from the screen flickered on his face.

"Got it!" he said. "I figured the other bidder had put in a top bid of five bucks. "Hang on a minute, and I'll finish up here."

Rhodes waited patiently. Ballinger had for years haunted garage sales around Blacklin County looking for old paperback books, the kind Ballinger claimed they didn't write anymore. Their virtues, according to Ballinger, were many: they were short, they were tough, they were well written.

"Not like those padded-out doorstops you see these days," he'd once told Rhodes. "Guys like Harry Whittington and Day Keene. Real pros. Those guys could tell more story in a hundred and twenty-eight pages than most people writing now can tell in a thousand."

But old paperback books were getting harder and harder to find. Go to a garage sale now, Ballinger said, and all you could see were historical romances, books by Koontz, King, and Grisham, and big fat techno-thrillers by Clancy and his clones, which were the kind of thing people wanted to read these days. But those weren't what Ballinger was looking for.

He turned away from the computer and looked up at Rhodes.

"Pretty good deal if you ask me," he said. "A copy of *Tokyo Doll* for only five-fifty."

Rhodes said he hadn't heard of that one.

"It's by John McPartland. Nobody's ever heard of him. Except me and whoever else was bidding on *Tokyo Doll*. But he was good. Trust me."

"I guess I'll have to," Rhodes said.

"The only thing is, I used to be able to get books like that for a dime at garage sales. Those days are gone forever."

"Like a lot of things," Rhodes said. "Listen, while I'm here, what about the autopsy report on Terry Don Coslin?"

"Dr. White sent it over to your office," Ballinger said. "How long are you going to try to keep this quiet?"

"I'm not trying to keep it quiet," Rhodes said. "I was just hoping the paper wouldn't find out about it in time to get it in today's edition."

"Well, they didn't," Ballinger said. "But they know now, and there's going to be a story tomorrow. It'll probably be in the Dallas papers before then, and I wouldn't be surprised if some of the TV people didn't start showing up tonight."

"Maybe the weather will keep them away," Rhodes said.

"Ha."

"Right. Nothing will keep them away. I guess I'll have to wrap things up before they get here."

"Any chance of you doing that?"

"Two," Rhodes said.

"Slim and none?"

"Those are the two."

"I don't think Dr. White found anything that's going to be much help to you, either."

"Just what I wanted to hear."

"But you never know," Ballinger said in an attempt to be encouraging. "He did mention that there was some little something that you were going to be interested in, but he didn't say what it was."

Rhodes wondered what it could have been. Maybe it was just as well he hadn't stayed in Obert. He was suddenly eager to read the report.

Ballinger turned back to the computer.

"I'm not trying to snub you," he said, "but there's a bid on a book by Charles Williams I want to check on."

"You go ahead," Rhodes told him. "I have to get on over to the jail anyway."

The rain had just about stopped, and there were no more eerie flashes of light inside the funeral home. Rhodes supposed that Blanton had finished up and left.

Rhodes got in the county car. Just as he started out of the driveway, the lights in the neighborhood all came back on.

Rhodes wondered if that was a good sign.

Probably not, he thought as he drove away.

28

▼

Lawton was nowhere around when Rhodes got back to the jail, but Hack was there, watching Oprah on his little TV set.

"Do you ever buy things from auctions on that computer?" Rhodes asked.

Hack turned off the TV set and said, "That wouldn't be right. I don't do stuff like that on county time. Besides, there's not anything on there that I want. Why?"

"Just wondering. Where's the autopsy report on Terry Don Coslin?"

"Right there on your desk," Hack said. "What about the ghost?"

"It didn't get Ballinger. He's fine."

"That's not what I meant."

Rhodes knew very well what Hack had meant, and he knew it was wrong to tease him, but he could never resist giving the dispatcher a dose of his own medicine.

"There wasn't any ghost," he said.

"I didn't think there was. But there must've been somethin'. What was it?"

"Just somebody taking pictures," Rhodes said, and went on to explain what the caller had seen.

"I don't blame that man's mama," Hack said when Rhodes was finished. "I think it's nice to have a picture of the deceased like that."

Rhodes didn't comment. He went over to his desk and located the report. Then he sat down, put on his glasses, and started to read.

There was nothing startling in the report at all. Terry Don had died from the effects of the fall, which had been obvious from the beginning. The interesting thing that Ballinger had mentioned was even smaller than Rhodes thought it would be. There had been some kind of mark across the top of Terry Don's right index finger, something almost like a rope burn but much smaller than any mark made by a rope would have been. For some reason, Rhodes thought he should know what the mark was, but the longer he thought about it, the less sure he became. All kinds of ideas were milling around in his head, but they weren't lining up in any logical order. He'd just have to wait until they did.

And the best thing to do while he was waiting was to go back to Obert and talk to a few more people.

The rain had stopped, but the clouds had hung on, heavy and dark. Rhodes had to use his headlights even though it was still a couple of hours until nightfall.

His first stop was Billy Quentin's house. As soon as Rhodes got out of the car, he could hear Grover barking out in back.

There was no sidewalk in Quentin's front yard, and in fact there wasn't much of a yard. It was mostly hard-packed dirt, which had turned slick and muddy in the rain. Rhodes could feel it sucking at his shoes as he walked to the porch.

Quentin, who must have been alerted by Grover's barking, came to the door before Rhodes could even knock. Quentin was again wearing a pair of overalls, but this time he had a T-shirt on with them, probably a concession to the fact that the rain had lowered the temperature considerably.

Rhodes was glad for the T-shirt because he now noticed that Quentin had enough back hair to stuff a pillow. Tufts of it stuck out above the collar of the T-shirt. Some of it was even sticking through the T-shirt.

Quentin also had thin lips and big ears. His ears were hairy, too. And he hadn't shaved that day. On him the scruffy look wasn't a fashion statement. Or if it was, it was saying all the wrong things.

"Oh," Quentin said when he saw Rhodes standing at his door. "It's you. The high sheriff."

"That's right. Can I come in?"

Quentin looked down at Rhodes's shoes, which had tracked mud up onto the porch.

"You really have to?" he said.

Rhodes scuffed his shoes against the porch, knocking most of the mud off.

"Yes," he said. "I really have to."

Quentin pushed the door open, and Rhodes entered. After he got a look inside, he wasn't really worried about his muddy shoes. Quentin wasn't going to win any awards for good house-keeping. There were newspapers lying on the floor and in the chairs, there were beer cans on the coffee table and on the TV set, there were pizza boxes on the floor, and there was an over-flowing ashtray by the couch. A football game was playing on the TV set, but there was no sound. Rhodes didn't know whether Quentin had the sound muted or whether he just preferred to watch without it.

The ashtray reminded Rhodes of the one in Terry Don's room, except that one had been empty. Rhodes wondered who had emp-tied it.

"Have a seat," Quentin said, moving to the couch, where there was one cleared cushion. He sat down, took a beer can off the coffee table, and had a drink. "Want a beer?"

"No, thanks," Rhodes said.

He pushed some newspapers out of a chair. They fluttered to the floor, and Rhodes sat down.

"Been watchin' the game," Quentin said, pointing to the television set with the hand that held the beer. "You like football?"

"I don't follow the pros much, except for the Cowboys," Rhodes said. "And I keep up with the Clearview Catamounts."

"Yeah? Well, you must not like 'em much, considerin' what you did to 'em last year."

People still blamed Rhodes for the Catamounts' unfortunate season, although it certainly hadn't been his fault one of the coaches got himself murdered. But Rhodes hadn't come to talk about that.

"I wanted to ask you a few things about Terry Don Coslin," he said.

"Don't know the gentleman," Quentin said, taking another sip of beer.

"You met him the other night, in your back yard."

"Oh, yeah, him. The one in the tight jeans. Tell you the truth, I'm surprised they didn't cut off his circulation. What about him?"

"Somebody killed him last night."

Quentin had been slouching on the couch, but now he straightened up and set the beer can back on the coffee table.

"I heard all the commotion up there at the college," he said. "I thought the whole place had blown up, and I watched the fire from out in the yard for a little while. But I was here at the house the whole time. I didn't have anything to do with that fire. And I sure as hell didn't kill anybody."

Rhodes wasn't entirely convinced of that. He said, "You didn't much like Coslin. You called him a window-peeper, and you wanted to shoot him."

Quentin rummaged around in the beer cans on the coffee table until he located a crumpled cigarette package and a matchbook. He straightened the pack and shook out a cigarette. He had to straighten that, too. When he was done, he stuck it in his mouth and lit it.

"I called him a window-peeper because he was one."

"You called me one, too," Rhodes reminded him.

"Yeah." Quentin exhaled smoke. "I was wrong about that, maybe. But that tight-pants guy, he was one for sure. Somebody woulda killed him sooner or later, but I wasn't the one who did it. And if I'd done it, you'd know it. I wouldn't just shoot him and run off. I'd stand my ground."

"He wasn't shot," Rhodes said.

"Well, there you are." Quentin ignored his overflowing ashtray and flipped ashes on his rug. "Must not've been me, then."

Rhodes didn't much like Quentin, and he didn't like his attitude. But he was beginning to believe that Quentin was telling the truth.

"You said he'd been on your property the other night," Rhodes said. "Before you took after him with the shotgun, I mean."

"Yeah, I said that. You didn't believe me, though. You asked me if I'd seen a naked woman, like I wouldn't know the difference in a woman and a man, even a long-haired sissy like that one. But I know the difference, all right. I wasn't always a dried-up little fart like I am now. I had me plenty of women, one time or another, by God."

"I don't think Coslin was a sissy," Rhodes said, deciding to let Quentin's last remark pass without comment.

"You got a right to your opinion," Quentin said. "I got a right to mine."

Rhodes stood up. Quentin didn't know it, but his criticisms of Coslin had given Rhodes something to think about, something that tied in with what Rhodes had already suspected.

"No need to rush off," Quentin said, clearly not meaning a word of it.

"Don't bother to get up," Rhodes said, as if Quentin would actually have made the gesture. "I can find my way out. And thanks for your help."

"Don't mention it," Quentin said, turning away, his eyes already focused on the soundless game.

29

▼

AFTER LEAVING QUENTIN'S PLACE, RHODES DROVE ON DOWN TO the Appleby house. The black clouds in the north were breaking up, and there were patches of red and orange showing through as the sun dropped down. By nightfall the sky would be clear and the weather turning colder.

Claude and his twin weren't home. They were still working at Wal-Mart. Mrs. Appleby was in the kitchen, cooking supper. Rhodes could smell the steak frying in the pan when he knocked on the door.

Mrs. Appleby invited him in and led him back to the kitchen. The steak was popping in grease in a skillet, and a little of the flour it had been rolled in was still lying on a piece of waxed paper on the counter.

"You're welcome to stay and have a bite to eat if you want to," Mrs. Appleby told Rhodes. "There's more than enough for you to have a plate. The boys should be here any minute."

Although his stomach was telling him to accept, Rhodes thought about all the barbecue he'd eaten for lunch. Not to mention the cobbler and ice cream.

"I'd love to stay," he said, "but I have too much to do. It does smell good, though."

The grease popped as Mrs. Appleby turned the steak with a two-tined fork. Rhodes thought about cream gravy and mashed potatoes.

"I just wanted to let you know that Claude did a really brave thing last night," Rhodes said. "If it hadn't been for him, I might have died in that building."

"I'm glad he was able to help you out," Mrs. Appleby said. "But I wish he hadn't been up there. He knows I don't like him or his brother rovin' over the countryside. They've been in trouble before, and if they don't look out, they'll be in trouble again. And after you helped 'em get those good jobs, too."

"I don't think Claude is going to get in any trouble," Rhodes said. "He wasn't doing any mischief."

Mrs. Appleby sniffed. "Well, you know best, bein' the sheriff. I just hope you're right."

Rhodes hoped so, too, but he wasn't entirely convinced. He still thought Claude was holding something back. He just didn't know what it was. But he was going to find out.

"I wanted to ask you about that person you saw," Rhodes said. "The one without any clothes on. You told me there were ways to know it was a woman, but you didn't say what those ways were."

"I guess you know what they are."

Rhodes realized he was treading on dangerous ground, but he forged ahead.

"I think I do, but, well, as I remember it, you said the woman was heading away from you, into the trees."

"That's right. That's what I said."

Mrs. Appleby wasn't going to give him any help, so Rhodes had to keep going. He said, "That's what I was wondering about, then. If she was heading away from you, how could you be sure it was a woman?"

"I told you," Mrs. Appleby said.

"You did?"

"There was that underwear, for one thing. No man I ever heard of would wear underwear like that."

Rhodes didn't even want to imagine Cy Appleby in bikini underwear. Especially not now that Cy was in prison.

"Besides," Mrs. Appleby said, "she had real long hair. You put the two together, and what do you have?"

Terry Don Coslin, Rhodes thought. *That's what you have.*

He said, "I'm not sure."

"Well, I am. No doubt about it, Sheriff, it was a naked woman runnin' around back there."

Rhodes wished that Claude were there. He wanted to ask if he'd gotten a front view of the "woman," but he was willing to bet that the answer would be no.

Rhodes said that he had to leave and that he appreciated Mrs. Appleby's help.

"You sure you can't stay? This steak is fryin' up just about right."

Rhodes's mouth watered at the prospect, but considering the barbecue and the cobbler, and considering that he still had a few people to talk to up at the college, he thanked her kindly and left before he weakened.

Rhodes wasn't sure that anyone would want to talk to him, but he hadn't reckoned with Claudia and Jan, who met him at the door of the dormitory and told him that although they were still working out the plot of their book, they had a couple of ideas they were sure he could use. Rhodes was becoming convinced that it wasn't just that everyone wanted to write a mystery novel; a lot of people also wanted to be detectives.

"I'd like to hear your ideas," he said. "But I have to talk to someone first."

"But you really need to hear about this," Claudia assured him. "It's a really great plot twist."

Rhodes resigned himself and said, "All right. Go ahead."

Both women looked around to see if anyone else was listening. No one was. All the other writers were intent on their own conversations. Some of them hadn't even noticed Rhodes come in.

"Here it is," Jan said when she was certain no one would overhear. "Suicide!"

"Suicide?" Rhodes said.

"Right," Claudia said. "Suicide. Get it?"

Rhodes had to admit that he didn't.

"It's simple," Jan said. "Henrietta, or whatever we'll be calling her in our book, kills herself because of her unrequited love for Terry Don. Or whatever we'll be calling him. And when Terry Don finds out what happened, he jumps to his death in remorse. Isn't it great?"

Rhodes didn't think it was so great. He didn't even think it was likely. Or even possible.

"How could someone kill herself by falling against a dresser?" he asked.

"Oh, it won't happen that way in the book," Claudia said. "She'll probably use poison. It's not as messy."

Rhodes said he didn't see how that was supposed to help him with the actual case. And he didn't see how it would help the book, either.

"You're writing a murder mystery without a murder," he said. "That wouldn't work."

"Maybe not in the book," Claudia admitted. "But what about here and now?"

"It's another angle to look at," Jan said. "It could have happened like that."

It could have, Rhodes thought, if Henrietta had poisoned herself, which she hadn't. He thanked the women for their ideas, though they seemed disappointed that he wasn't more enthusiastic, and went looking for Carrie Logan. He found her in her room, sitting at the tiny desk, and working on a notebook computer similar to the one Ballinger had been using.

The door was open, and Rhodes knocked on the facing. When Carrie looked up and saw him, her face colored.

"Hello, Sheriff," she said. "I was doing a little work on my book before dinner. We'll be eating in a few minutes, and I guess I really should be finishing up here. I'm running late already. I thought we'd be eating by now."

Rhodes hadn't thought about the evening meal and how it would be served. He asked Carrie.

"We're going to have sandwiches and things. French fries, maybe. They'll be bringing them here to the dorm, and we'll eat in our rooms."

"Then you don't have much to get ready for, do you," Rhodes said.

"Well, you know how it is. I have to save everything to a disk and shut down the computer and all that."

"I can wait," Rhodes said. "I want to talk to you for a minute when you're finished."

Carrie reddened again. She got a floppy disk from a briefcase on the floor and inserted it into the drive on the side of the computer. When she'd saved her work, she shut the computer down and closed it.

"I really do need to get ready for dinner," she said. "I hope this won't take long."

"It won't," Rhodes said. "I've been thinking about what you told me the other night, and I just wanted to ask you something about Vernell."

"Vernell and I were here in the room. We heard the yelling. That's really all I know."

"So you said. But I was wondering about something. You

didn't say anything until Vernell gave you a cue. It almost seemed as if she'd tipped you off about what she wanted you to say."

Carrie's face was getting redder all the time. She busied herself with putting her computer into the briefcase and avoided Rhodes's eyes.

"Are you saying I lied?" she asked, speaking to the floor.

"It's just something I was wondering about," Rhodes said. "In a case like this, I have to think things over and try to make sense out of them, and that's just one of the thoughts I've had."

"Well, you're w-wrong," Carrie said, her voice breaking.

Rhodes thought she might be going to cry, so he entered the room and closed the door. Carrie cringed as if she thought he might be about to attack her. He kept his distance so she wouldn't get too excited.

"Are you sure I'm wrong?" he asked. "You know that you could get in serious trouble if you're hampering the investigation of a murder, especially if you're withholding evidence."

He thought about Claude Appleby. He should have given him the same speech, but he was pretty sure it wouldn't have bothered Claude. He'd have to be handled differently.

"I—I'm not w—withholding anything," Carrie said.

She got up and went to a little nightstand between the room's twin beds and got a tissue from a box. She blew her nose and wiped her eyes.

"I think you are," Rhodes said. "I don't think Vernell was in the room, and I think you're covering up for her."

Carrie looked at him and started crying in earnest. Rhodes stood there and waited her out. After a while, she stopped crying, got another tissue, and wiped her eyes and cheeks.

"You're right," she said finally, her voice firmer as if she'd made some kind of decision. "I didn't want to lie, but Vernell told me it wouldn't hurt anything. I know she didn't kill Henrietta, no matter how much Henrietta hated her and no matter how many hateful things she said about her in that awful book she was writing."

"But Vernell wasn't in the room with you," Rhodes said.

"She was in here most of the time. But just before the yelling started, she had to go to the bathroom."

The dorm's two bathrooms were in the center of the hallway, so Vernell would have had to leave the room to get to them.

"So she could have killed Henrietta," Rhodes said. "When she was out of the room."

"No, no," Carrie said. "She wasn't gone long enough for that. I'm sure of it. She was just gone for a few seconds before it happened."

"A few seconds would've been enough," Rhodes said. "The door to Henrietta's room is just a step away."

"But she'd have had to go in there, get in a fight, and kill her. She wasn't gone that long. I just know it. I would never have said she was with me if I'd had any doubt at all. We were just trying to save her from unnecessary trouble."

"It didn't work," Rhodes said.

"I knew all along what we were doing was wrong, and I feel just awful about it. But I'm really sure Vernell is completely innocent. She's going to hate me for telling you this."

"She'll get over it," Rhodes said.

30

▼

So far, Rhodes thought, just about everyone he'd talked to had lied to him, except for maybe Jan and Claudia. And he wasn't too sure about them.

The lies, of course, had all been small ones, and all of them had been told for the best of reasons, at least in the mind of the tellers: to protect someone who otherwise might have fallen under suspicion. Or in some cases the lies had been for self-protection, which some people might have thought was an even better reason.

But in most investigations Rhodes had been involved in, he'd eventually seen through the lies and gotten to something that resembled the truth. This investigation wasn't shaping up to be any different.

And he did more than try to get the truth from people. While he was sorting through things, literally this time, in the case of Terry Don Coslin's dirty laundry, he was also running various scenarios through his head, trying to come up with one that fit all the facts. He thought he had a pretty good one for Henrietta's death now, one that took just about everything into account, but he still hadn't come up with a good idea of what might have happened to Terry Don. Maybe if he tested his first notion, he'd come up with something that would help him work out the rest of the sequence.

He walked down the hall to the dormitory's sitting room. There weren't enough chairs for everyone; many of the women were standing. Serena Thayer was talking to Belinda Marshall and Marian Willoughby, just as she had been at lunch.

Rhodes wondered if Belinda and Marian had teamed up to keep Serena away from Vernell. If they had, it was a good idea. Rhodes didn't feel like breaking up any more fights, and Serena seemed to be able to hold on to her temper when she was around the other two writers. Maybe that was because she liked them, or maybe it was because they knew better than to cross her. Rhodes didn't really care which. At least they were helping to keep Serena's temper in check.

Claudia and Jan were standing on the fringes of the conversation, listening avidly, as if in hopes that some of the basic precepts of successful writing might slip out. Rhodes was pretty sure they wouldn't, but you couldn't blame Claudia and Jan for hoping.

There were other small groups all around the room, and everyone was chattering away. The noise level was about like that of a third-grade classroom when the teacher has been gone for ten minutes or so.

Tom Chatterton came in through the front door while Rhodes was looking around for Vernell. Chatterton tried to get everyone's attention by clapping his hands, but for all the difference he made, he might as well have been patting two powder puffs together.

He looked at Rhodes over the heads of the women as if appealing for help. Rhodes shrugged. He wasn't going to fire off his pistol in the dormitory.

Jeanne Arnot was standing not far from Rhodes, talking earnestly to Lorene Winslow. Lorene was nodding her head and smiling, and Rhodes wondered if Jeanne was taking her on as a client. He hated to break into their discussion if that was the case. Lorene would never forgive him. On the other hand, Chatterton needed help.

Rhodes stepped over to Jeanne and tapped her on the shoulder. When she looked around, he said, loud enough for her to hear him over the din, "Do you have your whistle?"

She nodded and dug around in her purse. After a second or two she found it and brought it out, holding it where Rhodes could see it clipped to her key ring.

"Blow it," he said, and she did.

The shrill sound cut through all the conversations like a table saw through pine. It bounced off the walls and ceiling, and it was all Rhodes could do not to cover his ears.

The room grew very quiet as everyone looked at Jeanne, who stuffed the whistle and keys back into her purse.

"Thank you," Chatterton said loudly, calling attention to himself. "The Round-Up van is on the way with sandwiches for everyone. It will be here in about ten minutes, and"—he gave Serena a significant look—"there will be vegetarian sandwiches for anyone who requires them. You may eat in here, or you may eat in your rooms, wherever you'd be more comfortable. But wherever you eat, please clean up and put all the trash in the proper receptacles."

Rhodes was pretty sure he'd never heard anyone use the word *receptacles* before, and he was impressed.

"I thought they were going to be here before now," someone said.

"It must have taken them longer than they thought it would to get things ready," Chatterton said. "Or maybe they had trouble finding the vegetarian ingredients."

Serena Thayer broke away from Belinda and Marian and started elbowing her way in Chatterton's direction. Chatterton, being smart enough to use the word *receptacles* in a sentence, was also smart enough to know when he'd gone too far. He started backing toward the door as Rhodes tried to get himself in position to block Serena's path.

He did, but she didn't want to stop. She came to a halt directly in front of him, almost touching his chest, with her eyes staring almost directly into his. He hadn't realized until now how tall she was.

He knew, however, how bad her temper was, and he wasn't surprised that she was almost vibrating with anger.

"Let me at him," she said.

Rhodes wondered if she'd use a line like that in one of her books. Probably not, he decided.

"I think you should relax," he said. "Why don't we go outside and have a little talk."

Serena took a deep breath, let it out slowly, and said, "Why Sheriff, how gallant. But I have to warn you that my heart belongs to another."

Rhodes liked that line, too. She'd probably actually used that one. Or maybe not. Rhodes hadn't read enough romance novels to be sure.

"I don't have romance on my mind," he said.

"I'm sure you don't. If I know you, you have murder on your mind."

Claudia had made her way to them by then, and Rhodes could almost see the lightbulb flash on over her head. She reached into her purse and brought out her notebook and pen. Rhodes thought he knew exactly what she was writing down. It was the title of the mystery novel she and Jan were working on: *Murder on His Mind*, which he had to admit had a nice ring to it. Claudia was certainly getting her money's worth from the workshop.

Rhodes took Serena's elbow and escorted her outside. The sky was inky black, full of the stars Terry Don had been admiring not so long ago, and the night was getting cool.

"Very romantic," Serena said, looking up at the stars and then back at Rhodes. "Are you married, Sheriff?"

"As a matter of fact, I am."

"Too bad. But then you warned me you didn't have romance in mind."

"That's right. I want to ask you something about Terry Don."

"And what might that be?"

"You seem to have known him pretty well, and you knew Henrietta had a crush on him. You didn't really mention how he felt about her."

"He thought the book was funny. I told you that."

"But the book and the woman aren't the same thing."

"You're pretty insightful for a hick-town sheriff. You'd be surprised at how many people don't understand that."

"I'd think it would be obvious," Rhodes said.

"Well, it isn't."

"I'll take your word for it. Now, tell me about Coslin and Henrietta."

"He didn't really say much about her. He did mention that they were a hot item when they were in high school. Maybe he still sort of liked her, even if he didn't say so. But he could never be serious about any one woman. He liked women too much to let himself get tied down to just one of them."

"But if she'd invited him to her room, he might have gone."

Serena laughed. She had a nice laugh, one that didn't seem to go with her temper.

"He'd have gone to anybody's room. I liked Terry Don, Sheriff. I liked him a lot. But I wasn't under any illusions about his character, thank God. And, as I said, I'm not the jealous type."

"Not even of Jeanne Arnot?"

"You know about her and Terry Don?"

"All I know is what I read in Henrietta's book."

"It's probably true. But even if it is, I don't care. Jeanne's my agent, and she makes a lot of money for me. What Terry Don does is his own business."

Serena shivered as if from the cold and moved closer to Rhodes, so close that their shoulders were touching. Serena definitely wasn't cold.

"What about your wife?" she asked. "Is she the jealous type?"

"I think so," Rhodes said. "And she's licensed to carry a handgun."

That wasn't true, but it seemed to Rhodes like a good idea to say it.

"Oh, my. A real Texas cowgirl."

"Not exactly," Rhodes said.

Serena moved even closer. Rhodes stood his ground, though he thought he might be making a mistake.

"You know, Sheriff," Serena said, "you don't seem to like me much, but I think we could get along if we'd just try a little harder."

Rhodes didn't ask what she had in mind. He said, "I don't think it's a good idea to get too friendly with people involved in a murder investigation."

Serena moved away from him, and her voice turned hard.

"You think I killed that little bitch, don't you."

There was another line that Rhodes was pretty sure Serena had never used in one of her books.

"You're wrong about that," Rhodes said. "I don't think you killed her."

"You don't?"

"That's what I said."

"Then why did you get me off to myself out here and let me waste my feminine wiles on you? I thought you were going to handcuff me and cart me off to the jail."

"I just wanted to ask you something."

"And that's all?"

"That's all."

Serena didn't look as if she believed him. She said, "Let me ask you something first."

"Go ahead."

"Would you have shot me last night?"

"Of course not."

"But you pointed a gun at my head."

"I pointed it *over* your head. I haven't shot too many people, and I wouldn't want to add you to the list."

"Thank you. I guess."

"You're welcome. Now what about letting me ask *my* questions?"

"It's your turn."

"Good," Rhodes said, but then he changed his mind about asking. He had something he wanted to tell her first.

He was about to say it when the van from the Round-Up appeared. It stopped in front of the dormitory, and Sam Blevins got out of the cab.

"Seems like you're always around at mealtimes, Sheriff," he said. "I'll be glad to give you a sandwich if you want one. Sell you one, I mean."

"I might take you up on that," Rhodes said. "Later."

"There'll be plenty," Blevins said.

Two more men joined him. They opened the back doors of the van and began unloading large covered trays. They handed one to Blevins, who carried it inside. The men followed him in with another tray and a large plastic bag full of smaller bags of potato chips.

"You were going to ask me something," Serena reminded Rhodes.

"That's right, but first I want to say that nearly everyone I've talked to here has lied to me because they wanted to give someone else an alibi for the time of Henrietta's murder. I don't think you're the exception."

Serena batted her eyes, a tactic that Rhodes thought would have been more effective had the light been better.

"Why, Sheriff," she said. "Whatever do you mean?"

"You vouched for Jeanne Arnot. But I've been thinking about it, and what the two of you said didn't seem quite right."

"Why not? It sounded fine to me."

"Jeanne said something about how you didn't mind if she smoked, and she implied that you were with her. You didn't contradict her, but you never actually said that you were with her. I think that's because she was smoking outside the building, and you were inside it."

"There's no smoking inside," Serena said.

"I know that. But that's not the point."

"What's the point, then?"

"The point is that you weren't with Jeanne when you said you were."

"What if I wasn't?"

"That's an easy one. Then she was somewhere else."

"Oh, all right. It doesn't matter, I suppose. You're right. She was outside, smoking a cigarette. But she'd been talking to me just a few minutes earlier, so I know she didn't kill anybody. She couldn't just walk away from a conversation with me and go kill a woman."

"Maybe," Rhodes said.

He wished he could remember if Jeanne had walked up to the fight between Serena and Vernell after it was all over. If she had, she might possibly have been in the main building with Terry Don and might be the key to the whole thing. But Rhodes hadn't been in a position to see who came strolling up to join the crowd.

And then he realized that it didn't matter. Everything unknotted in his head, and he was almost sure he knew what had happened to both Henrietta and Terry Don. The answers had been there all along, but they'd all been kinked and tangled, like knots in a rope. But now it was as if Rhodes had tied the rope to one thing and pitched it away from him. As it glided through the air, all the knots and kinks disappeared. And when it landed, it lay perfectly straight between one point and the other.

"Sheriff?" Serena said, waving a hand in front of his eyes. "What are you looking at?"

"A picture," Rhodes said.

"A picture? Of what?"

"A killer," he told her.

31

▼

RHODES LEFT SERENA STANDING IN FRONT OF THE DORMITORY and went back inside. Blevins had set the sandwich trays on a table, and everyone had helped herself. Rhodes could see that some of the sandwiches had ham on them, and some had what looked like roast beef. As far as he could tell, there weren't any vegetarian specials. Several people were sitting there eating and chatting, but the others were all in their rooms, or visiting in the rooms of friends.

Rhodes went down the hall to Vernell's room. The door was open, and Carrie and Vernell were sitting on their beds, eating ham sandwiches and potato chips out of small bags.

"I have to talk to Vernell," Rhodes told Carrie, who gave him a stricken look.

"I haven't told her yet," she said.

"Told me what?" Vernell asked.

"Nothing," Rhodes said. "Why don't you go to the front room, Carrie, and eat with some of the others."

Carrie stood up with her sandwich in her hand, but she looked as if she'd lost all interest in eating it. There was a can of Dr

Pepper on the nightstand, and she took that, as well. Then she walked out of the room without another word. She left the bag of potato chips behind.

"What's going on, Sheriff?" Vernell asked.

Rhodes closed the door and sat down on the bed opposite Vernell.

"We have to talk about Henrietta," he said. "I think there are some things you need to tell me."

Vernell put her half-eaten sandwich beside a can of Pepsi that sat on a napkin on the nightstand.

"I don't think so," she said. "I've already told you everything I know."

"Then I'll tell you something," Rhodes said. "Here's the way I think it happened."

"Wait," Vernell said. "Are you accusing me of murder?"

"No. I think it was an accident."

Vernell looked relieved, but she didn't reach for her Pepsi. She said, "You're right. It was an accident. It could have happened to anyone."

"But if it was an accident," Rhodes went on, "why didn't you just say so?"

"Because . . . because it might have hurt someone."

"You," Rhodes said. "It might have hurt you."

Vernell sat up a little straighter. She looked a lot less relieved than she had only seconds before.

"Just hold on, now, Sheriff," she said. "What are you saying? Do you think I killed Henrietta?"

"I didn't say that."

"You sure were coming close."

"Not exactly. I was just wondering if I was right about you. And I think I am."

"How do you mean? I didn't kill anybody!"

"You did something just as bad, though, didn't you."

"I don't know what you're talking about!"

"I think you do. You didn't kill Henrietta, but you saw who did. And you didn't tell me. You got Carrie to lie for you instead."

Vernell looked at the closed door. She said, "Damn that Carrie! I should have known she couldn't keep her mouth shut."

"She didn't want to tell me," Rhodes said. "And she didn't really have to. I already knew she was lying."

"You can't prove that."

"I think I can. Let me tell you what you saw. Then you can tell me if I'm right."

Vernell just stared at him, looking stubborn as a statue.

"You told Carrie that you had to go to the bathroom," Rhodes said. "Maybe that's true, or maybe it's not. Maybe you heard something in Henrietta's room and wanted to get your ear to the door to hear it a little better. Your room is certainly close enough for you to have heard something."

"I went to the bathroom," Vernell said. "And that's the truth. I was in there when the yelling started, and that's the truth, too."

"I guess that's possible," Rhodes said. "But if it's true, you didn't stay in the bathroom. You came out in time to see someone leaving the building through that back door."

Vernell dropped her eyes and looked for her Pepsi. She picked it up, brought it to her mouth, then put it back down on the napkin without taking a drink.

"I didn't see the killer," she said. "Besides, it was an accident, like you said."

"If you didn't see the killer," Rhodes said, "who did you see?"

"Jeanne Arnot."

"That's what I thought," Rhodes said.

"How did you know?"

"She took you on as a client. She said she could get you a lot of money for your next book. Chatterton told me that everyone knows about it."

"What does that prove?"

"It doesn't prove anything. She could have wanted you for a client because you've written a really wonderful book. But the timing would seem to indicate that it might be something else."

"I *have* written a wonderful book," Vernell said. "You'll see."

"I read your first one, and it wasn't bad," Rhodes said. "It was pretty good, in fact. But it didn't make a lot of money, did it?"

"I didn't have Jeanne Arnot as an agent then. It would have done a lot better if I had."

"You're not going to have her now, either," Rhodes said.

"Oh, yes I am. She promised."

"It won't be an easy promise for her to keep, though."

"Why not?"

"Because," Rhodes said, "she's going to be in prison."

Rhodes left Vernell sitting in the room with her sandwich and Pepsi and started back to the front of the dorm. While he was still in the hallway, he saw Carrie Logan, who was heading straight for him, still crying. Or crying again. Her head was down, and she didn't see Rhodes. The hall was too narrow for him to get out of the way, and she was coming too fast for him to back up. So she ran right into him.

Rhodes had been able to brace himself, so he didn't fall. He didn't even move much. Maybe a step backward, but that was all.

Carrie looked up at him. Her eyes were red, and her makeup was a mess.

"What's the matter now?" Rhodes asked.

"Oh, S-Sheriff. It's all my f-fault. I shouldn't have said anything, but I didn't know it would make any d-difference. And now she's run off."

"Who's run off?"

"The p-person Vernell saw in the hall, I guess. I d-didn't mean to warn her. I just said that you were t-talking to Vernell about it, and she ran out the front d-door."

Carrie was still talking when Rhodes shoved past her, but he could no longer hear a word she said. He had his mind on other things.

The way Rhodes had worked it out, Henrietta and Terry Don had arranged a little get-together in her room. While Lorene was talking to the writers, Henrietta would be fulfilling her high-school dreams.

But Jeanne Arnot must have noticed that Terry Don had slipped away, and she'd gone to find him, either to see if she could fulfill some dreams of her own or to be sure he didn't fulfill those of anyone else.

Maybe she'd even spent a few minutes waiting in his room and smoking a cigarette that she'd tamped out in the ashtray, which she'd then dumped into the toilet and flushed away. At any rate, by the time she'd located Terry Don, he was already halfway to doing what Henrietta wanted. Jeanne must have gotten into the room, but by that time Terry Don had slipped out the window and started on his way, his clothes tucked underneath his arm.

He'd gotten sidetracked, however, before he could sneak back to his own room, by Tom Chatterton, who'd been leaving the president's house and going over to the dorm. Terry Don hadn't been to Obert in years, if he'd ever been there even when he lived in Clearview, so it was easy enough for him to go astray while trying to avoid Chatterton and wander down behind the Appleby and Quentin houses, where he'd been seen running around in his skivvies and mistaken for a woman because of his long hair and his peculiar taste in underwear. Or at least it seemed peculiar to Rhodes and to Mrs. Appleby. In his haste to get back to where he belonged, Terry Don had dropped a sock, the one Rhodes had found later, and the one Terry Don had gone back to look for when Quentin decided to ventilate him with the shotgun.

Jeanne Arnot was the one who'd argued with Henrietta and perhaps shoved her down, with the result that Henrietta had a serious depressed fracture of the skull and wouldn't be writing any more manuscripts. Jeanne had then left by the back door and come in through the front as if she'd been at the main building all along, but Vernell had seen her leaving Henrietta's room and used that fact to get herself a literary agent and the promise of a fat book contract in the future if things worked out.

Terry Don must have had an inkling of what happened between Jeanne and Henrietta, and Jeanne had shoved him out the window of the main building. Rhodes was sure of that part, though he didn't yet know just why. He was planning to ask Jeanne about all that.

He should have realized that Jeanne had pushed Terry Don when he had seen the whistle on the key ring. It had been on a chain earlier, and Rhodes was betting that Terry Don had grabbed the chain and broken it as he fell, causing the burn on his index finger. And leaving a tiny link of the chain in the crack in the main building's third floor. Jeanne had either found the link after bashing Rhodes in the head with a bucket, or she'd tried to dispose of it by blowing up the building.

Rhodes would have liked to know what had happened to the rest of the chain. Did Jeanne have it, all except for a link or two, or had Terry Don carried it down with him? If he had, someone had taken it from his dead hand.

Rhodes thought it was just barely possible that Claude Appleby might have done that. Claude had, after all, been pretty reluctant to talk about what he had or hadn't seen, had or hadn't done.

Or maybe Jeanne had gotten the chain back.

If he ever caught up with her, Rhodes thought, he'd ask her

about that, too. But catching up with her might be a problem. Carrie had tipped her off, and Rhodes had no idea where she had gone.

When Rhodes got to the front room, it was buzzing with talk. Rhodes couldn't make out any individual words because there were no more small-group conversations. Even though he didn't know what was being said, Rhodes figured that people were talking about Jeanne Arnot's sudden departure. Everyone was talking to everyone else all at the same time, except for Chatterton, who saw Rhodes and shoved his way over.

"What's going on, Sheriff?" he yelled.

"Jeanne Arnot!" Rhodes yelled back, without explaining. "Where'd she go?"

"Outside, but—"

Rhodes didn't wait to hear the rest. He pushed through the crowd, oblivious to the looks he was getting from those he elbowed and shoved. When he got outside, he looked around for Jeanne, but he didn't see her anywhere.

As he tried to spot the runaway agent, Rhodes remembered the last time he'd chased down a killer in Obert. He'd been in his car for a while, zinging along the county roads, and when he'd gotten out of the car, he'd been attacked by the killer, who'd commandeered the county tree whacker. It hadn't been a good experience, and Rhodes hoped the tree whacker was nowhere around.

It was pretty likely that Jeanne didn't have a car, Rhodes thought. Someone would have had to pick her up at the airport in Waco or Dallas and drive her to Obert. Which meant that she must be on foot. There was nowhere she could go on foot, unless she walked to the highway and tried to hitch a ride, or unless she wandered in the wrong direction, the way Terry Don had done when he'd left Henrietta's room. It was easy for someone from the city to get disoriented in a place like Obert's Hill where there was only one landmark and where every direction was down.

Rhodes looked toward the road to town and saw no one. He looked at the road that ran past the main building and down the hill past Quentin's house. He didn't see anyone there, either.

Then he heard a dog barking, and almost immediately after that, he heard a shotgun.

32

▼

Rhodes took off down the hill, making the best time he could. He was hampered both by the darkness and by the fact that he was still sore from the previous night's adventures, but he made pretty good time since he knew more or less where he was going. Otherwise, he would have been in serious trouble, because the sky was cloudy and there were no lights to help him. The glow in the dormitory windows reached no farther than the grass just outside the building.

The shotgun boomed again, and in the silence that returned after its blast had stopped echoing, Rhodes could hear Grover barking away. Rhodes had to give Grover credit. He was always on the alert.

The shotgun thundered again, and Rhodes tried to pick up his pace. He didn't want Billy Quentin to kill Jeanne, though considering his accuracy so far, it seemed unlikely that he was going to hit her. You never knew with a shotgun, though. The buckshot spread out quickly after a certain distance, and Rhodes had heard of cases where one little piece of shot in just the wrong place had been enough to kill someone.

So he started yelling for Quentin to stop shooting.

"This is the sheriff!" he shouted. "Don't shoot!"

Quentin was apparently determined not to allow any more sneaking window-peepers on his property whether they were doing any actual peeping or whether they included the sheriff within their ranks. He fired off another round.

"Quentin!" Rhodes yelled. "Put down that gun or I'll arrest you for reckless endangerment and attempted murder!"

Quentin either wasn't paying attention, didn't care, or figured that dead men couldn't arrest anyone. He kept right on blasting away, and in between the shots Grover kept on barking. Half the people in Obert must have been aroused by now, or they would have been had they lived within hearing distance. One advantage of a sparse population is that sometimes your nearest neighbors were half a mile away.

Rhodes's feet were getting heavy from mud he'd picked up as he ran, and he was slowing down more and more. That was probably a good thing, he thought, as he was getting very close to Quentin's place. He came to a stop behind a tree, hoping that Quentin couldn't hear him panting. It was unlikely that he could, thanks to Grover, who by this time had worked himself into a positive frenzy of barking, so Rhodes leaned forward with his hands on his knees and tried to catch his breath. He wondered why Grover wasn't panting. He seemed able to bark continuously without ever having to pause to breathe.

After a few seconds, Rhodes realized that although Grover was still barking, Quentin was no longer shooting. Rhodes thought that was a good thing. He called out, "Quentin, this is Sheriff Rhodes. I'm right here by the house, and I'm going to show myself. Have you put that gun down?"

There was no answer. Rhodes took another breath or two and said, "Quentin? Are you still there?"

Again there was no reply. Rhodes was beginning to wonder whether Quentin was all right. He hadn't looked like a candidate for a heart attack, being skinny and wiry, but Rhodes knew you couldn't always tell about a man's cholesterol level by his appearance.

"Quentin?" Rhodes said, stepping from behind the tree.

As soon as he stepped out of the dark shadow of the tree, the shotgun blasted and Rhodes heard the shot ripping through the leaves of the tree and ticking off the branches. Something tugged at his shirtsleeve.

Rhodes hit the ground and hugged it. He had a feeling he knew what had happened, but he had no idea *how* it had. Jeanne Arnot had somehow gotten hold of the shotgun.

Rhodes wondered how many rounds had been fired. Had Quentin reloaded? Rhodes tried to count back. Four? Five? Six? Rhodes wasn't sure.

Quentin must have reloaded, he thought, but if he hadn't, did Jeanne Arnot know how?

And if she did, did she have access to any cartridges?

At least one thing was explained. Rhodes knew now why Grover was having such a fit. Quentin wasn't there to tell him to be quiet.

Well, Rhodes thought, that probably wasn't quite true. Quentin was there, all right. He just wasn't in any condition to say anything to his dog. Or to anyone else.

Rhodes started to inch forward on his stomach. There was no telling where Jeanne Arnot might be or whether she had any ammunition left, and he certainly couldn't hear her, thanks to Grover, whose lungs must have been made of some form of highly flexible leather. He was full of energy, too. Every now and then, in the minuscule space of silence between barking fits, Rhodes could hear the jingling of a chain-link fence as Grover threw himself against it.

When he reached another tree, Rhodes stood up and took cover behind it. He pulled out his pistol and checked it. He didn't want to shoot Jeanne, but she didn't know that. Maybe she'd give up when she learned that he was armed.

"Jeanne!" he said, careful to stay behind the tree. "This is Sheriff Rhodes. I know the shotgun is out of shells. Put it down, and we can talk."

The part about knowing the gun was out of shells was a lie, but Rhodes was willing to take the chance that Jeanne would believe him.

She didn't. There was a roar, and buckshot ripped into the tree trunk, tearing away the bark and several sizable chunks of wood. Jeanne was a definite hazard to the environment, and she must not have been very far away. And she clearly didn't plan to talk to him.

Rhodes would have to wait her out, and he would have, except that he wasn't very good at waiting in certain situations. This was one of them.

He saw another tree not far away, maybe ten feet, so he ran for it, arriving safely and with no shots being fired.

Grover didn't like it, though. The rapid movement seemed to irritate him exceedingly and to give him a second wind. He barked and carried on even more than before, if that was possible, hurling himself at the fence with renewed enthusiasm.

Rhodes looked out from behind the tree. He didn't see anyone, but there were so many shadows that someone could have been standing within a couple of yards of him and he might not have known it.

Grover knew it. He barked and rattled the fence fiercely. Rhodes was tempted to tell him to calm down, but it wouldn't have helped, and it would have revealed his position if Jeanne Arnot hadn't figured it out yet.

Rhodes was still trying to decide what to do when he heard someone calling his name. It wasn't Jeanne. It was Claude Appleby.

"Sheriff, are you around here somewhere?"

"Over here," Rhodes said. "But be careful. There's a woman out there with a shotgun."

"Not anymore," Claude said. "She's gone."

"What about Billy Quentin?"

"He's here," Claude said. "He looks like he might be dead, though."

Rhodes sighed, holstered his pistol, and stepped out from behind the tree.

"Let's have a look," he said, walking over to where Claude was looking down at something on the ground.

The something was Billy Quentin, who was lying on his back, his eyes closed. He looked dead, all right, but there was a thick tree branch lying nearby, and Rhodes thought that maybe it had been used on Quentin the way the bucket had been used on Rhodes. Jeanne Arnot had a way of sneaking up on you.

Rhodes knelt down and checked for a pulse in Quentin's neck. It was beating strongly.

"He'll be okay," Rhodes told Claude, speaking loudly so as to be heard over the sound of Grover's constant barking. "Unless he has a skull fracture or a concussion. What are you doing here?"

Claude looked down at his shoes as if they were very interesting, although they were only cheap running shoes that he'd most likely bought in the Wal-Mart shoe department.

"I was out walking around," he said. "And I heard the shooting. I started not to come over here, but then I figured I'd like to know what was going on."

"And you saw the woman," Rhodes said. "Did she happen to see you?"

"I'm not sure." Claude looked up. "She ran off, though, and she was carrying a shotgun."

"I have to find her," Rhodes said.

"What about that dog?" Claude said. "If we let him out,

maybe he'd track her down. He seems pretty upset about every-thing."

"He might track her," Rhodes said. "Or he might just bite us."

"Naw, not old Grover. He wouldn't hurt a fly. He just likes to make noise."

"You seem to know him pretty well."

"You know how it is," Claude said. "You make friends with a dog, and he won't bark at you."

"If you happen to be going for a walk after dark, you mean."

"Yessir."

"Well, never mind that. Let him out. We'll see what happens."

Claude went over to the pen, which got Grover even more excited than before, if that was possible. When Claude opened the gate, Grover flew out of it like a furry ballistic missile, nearly knocking Rhodes down. He was shaggy and of indeterminate ancestry. It looked to Rhodes as if he had somehow inherited the least attractive aspects of all their appearances. But he didn't bite anyone.

And he didn't go after Jeanne Arnot. He went straight to Quentin and started licking his face.

"I guess he likes him," Rhodes said.

"Looks that way," Claude said. "He's not going to be much help in tracking that woman after all. But maybe you won't need him."

Quentin was beginning to stir around under Grover's lapping tongue. He hadn't opened his eyes, however, so Rhodes couldn't hold up two fingers to test him for a concussion.

"Which way did the woman go?" Rhodes asked Claude.

Claude pointed west and said, "Down toward Obert's Creek. That's why you might not need the dog."

"I know what you mean," Rhodes said.

*   *   *

Benjamin Franklin Obert, an obscure pioneer, might or might not have had a considerable ego, but he had been the first person to settle down on a particular Texas hill, and for that reason his name was attached to any number of things: to the hill itself, to the little town that grew up near where he built his home, to the college that had later been built in the town, and to the sluggish little creek that flowed around the bottom of the hill.

Or it flowed most of the time. When the summers were very dry, it occasionally disappeared altogether, leaving behind only a muddy bottom that eventually dried out, became hard, and cracked crazily.

It was now flowing about as much as it ever did, thanks to the earlier rainstorm and to several others that had passed through the area earlier in the month. The area around it was boggy and full of frogs, bugs, and the occasional snake. Rhodes wasn't fond of snakes. For that matter, he didn't much like bugs, either. Frogs didn't bother him.

He wondered how Jeanne Arnot felt about them. That was another thing he could ask her when he caught up with her.

If he ever did.

"You stay here with Mr. Quentin," he told Claude.

"If Ma and Clyde heard the shootin', they'll be over here before long," Claude said. "They could take care of Mr. Quentin, and I could go with you to help out."

"You're not a deputy," Rhodes said. "So you stay here. Anyway, I have another job for you. When your mother gets here, you go back to your house and call for an ambulance. Then call the jail and tell Mr. Jensen to send Ruth Grady out here as fast as he can. You got all that?"

"Yessir," Claude said. "What about that dog? You want me to put him back in the pen?"

Rhodes looked at Grover, who was still washing Quentin's face.

"Don't bother him," Rhodes said. "No need to start him barking again."

"Right," Claude said.

When he was still a good fifty yards from the creek, Rhodes was slogging through mud that came up to the tops of his socks. Every time he took a step, there was a loud sucking sound before the gooey muck flowed back together. He'd heard several frogs and been bitten by more than several bugs, but he hadn't encountered any snakes.

And he hadn't encountered Jeanne Arnot, either. It occurred to him in mid-slog that she'd outsmarted him all the way around.

Jeanne had gone down the hill, but that didn't mean she had to stay there. If she hadn't run across Quentin, she would probably have started back up a whole lot sooner, but Quentin had distracted her for a while.

She might have been expecting Rhodes. She might even have had the tree branch ready for him instead of Quentin, who'd fouled up her plans temporarily. But then Claude had shown up, and she'd been quick to take advantage. She let him see her running off in one direction, while planning all the time to go make a quick turn back to where she'd come from.

Either that, or she was hiding somewhere up to her nose in mud and sludge. Somehow Rhodes didn't think that was the case. He looked back up the hill to where the lights in the dormitory showed up brightly in the darkness. He pulled a foot out of the ooze and started in that direction.

Once he was onto more solid ground, he broke into a heavy trot, but he didn't make very good time. Not only were his feet weighed down with mud, but his pants legs were soaked and slimy. He hoped Jeanne was as big a mess as he was, though he didn't think she would be. She was smarter than he was, and she wouldn't have gotten as close to the creek as he did.

He was about halfway up the hill when he heard a commotion from the dormitory. He sped up his trot as much as he could, which wasn't much.

He didn't think he was going to get there in time, and he was right. By the time he reached the dorm, Jeanne was already there, and she still had the shotgun.

There was one other little problem, as well.

She also had Vernell.

33

▼

Vernell wasn't happy. In fact, she looked so upset that Rhodes thought she might have exploded if it had been possible for a person to do that. Her face was as red as if she had been holding her breath for four or five minutes. Maybe she had, though it didn't seem likely. Rhodes wondered if she was still as pleased with her agent as she had been when they'd worked out whatever deal they had.

Probably not, since Rhodes doubted that at the time Jeanne had been gripping Vernell's hair with one hand and holding a shotgun barrel under her chin with the other.

Jeanne herself looked harried but in control, while everyone else just looked surprised. Now that the fuss had died down, no one was saying a word. They were all staring at Jeanne and Vernell.

Rhodes looked at Jeanne's legs. She was wearing denim pants, and they didn't appear wet at all. He'd been right about her. She hadn't gone anywhere near the creek.

"Hello, Sheriff," Jeanne said when Rhodes walked up. "I was hoping it might take you a little longer to get here."

"I rushed," Rhodes said. "You aren't planning to shoot Vernell, are you?"

"I'd hate to have to do that," Jeanne said. "But I suppose it's all up to you."

"How's that?"

"It depends on what kind of deal we can work out," Jeanne said.

Vernell chose that moment to try to wriggle loose. She jerked her head to the left and twisted her body in the other direction. It might have worked if Jeanne hadn't been expecting something. As it was, Vernell just got her head jerked back into place and got her chin jabbed by the shotgun.

"You shouldn't do that," Jeanne said. "My finger might slip, and that would make a mess all over everything."

"I'm afraid there wouldn't be any deal if that happened," Rhodes said, though he didn't think there would be one in any event.

"True," Jeanne said, "but there might be some satisfaction in it. I really get tired of people who try to take advantage of me."

Rhodes wondered who she might mean, aside from Vernell, that is. Maybe she felt that way about all her clients.

"What is it that you want?" he asked. "Exactly."

"I don't suppose you'd just let me go."

"No," Rhodes said. "I'm pretty sure we couldn't work that out."

"So it's really hard for me to decide what to do," Jeanne said. "Things don't look too good for me right now."

Rhodes didn't have anything to say to that. She had summed up the situation pretty well.

"So I guess I'll have to tell you the truth," she said. "The problem is that I didn't do what you think I did. That's why I think you could let me go and not worry about it."

"How do you know what I think you did?"

"Carrie hinted at it. I figured out the rest. I know I should have told you, but I didn't think you'd believe me. By the time I figured everything out, it was too late to try to convince you. Now I have to try."

"Go ahead, then," Rhodes said. "If you didn't kill Henrietta, who did?"

"I should think that would be obvious," Jeanne said.

"Not to me."

"Why do you think I took this woman prisoner?" Jeanne asked. "Because I wanted a hostage?"

"The thought had crossed my mind."

"Well, you can forget it. She's a killer. And I'm holding her for you."

Vernell gave Rhodes a wild look, and Rhodes pretended to think things over for a few seconds. Then he said, "You know, I can see how it could've been that way. Vernell has been covering up. I'm going to ask everybody to go inside except for you and me and Vernell. Then we can talk things over. Does that sound fair?"

Jeanne said that it did, and Rhodes told everyone to go inside. He had to tell them twice before anyone would move. Rhodes thought they were all a little disappointed that Jeanne hadn't pulled the trigger, and they were hoping that if they stayed, she might do it.

But finally Claudia took over. She said, "Come on, now, everybody. Let's do what the sheriff says and let him work things out. It's not any of our business."

Rhodes could tell that at least half of them did think it was their business, especially Serena, Belinda, and Marian, who must have been hoping for some good specific details for the mystery novels they were planning to write in order to escape being pegged as romance writers. And Chatterton, who looked stricken by the whole thing. But after a few seconds of grumbling, everyone went back into the dorm, where most of them stood peering out the door and windows.

"Now what?" Jeanne asked.

"Now you tell me how Vernell killed Henrietta," Rhodes said.

The way Jeanne explained it, things had happened just about as Rhodes had suspected, except that it had been Vernell who got into Henrietta's room, scared off Terry Don, and got into some kind of argument with Henrietta.

"It had something to do with a radio contest," Jeanne said. "I'm not sure of the details."

All through the recounting of the story, Vernell got redder and redder. By the time Jeanne had finished, Vernell's face was roughly the color of a wild-cherry cough drop. But she couldn't do or say anything because the shotgun was pressed so firmly against her chin that she couldn't open her mouth. Rhodes had a feeling that Jeanne was going to pull the trigger accidentally any second now if he didn't do something to prevent it.

"What you say all fits," Rhodes told Jeanne. "Now that you've explained it, I can see that I was wrong about just about everything. But that still leaves one question. Who killed Terry Don Coslin?"

"I don't know the answer to that," Jeanne said. "But then I'm not the sheriff here. You'll have to figure it out for yourself. Maybe it was Vernell."

At that, Vernell tensed. Rhodes hoped she wouldn't struggle because Jeanne's finger was even more tense than Vernell. Rhodes was sure that Vernell was within a millimeter of getting her head blown off while trying to escape.

Then he saw headlights approaching. There was no siren, no lightbar flashing, so it wasn't the ambulance, though that would be coming along any minute. It was Ruth Grady, who stopped her county car and got out.

She looked the situation over and said, "Need any help here, Sheriff?"

"I don't think so," Rhodes told her. "We're going to have to arrest Vernell for murder. That's about it."

"Who did she kill?"

"Henrietta," Rhodes said. "And maybe Terry Don."

"What about that shotgun?"

"Ms. Arnot's just about to give that to me," Rhodes said, reaching out. In the distance he heard the ambulance siren yowling.

Jeanne heard it, too, and she took her eyes off Rhodes for a fraction of a second.

As soon as she did, Rhodes took two steps forward and grabbed the shotgun just as Jeanne pulled the trigger.

34

▼

VERNELL FELL BACKWARD, JEANNE'S HAND STILL TANGLED IN her hair. Luckily for Vernell, Rhodes had managed to jerk the shotgun from under her chin, so Vernell's head was still attached to her body.

Rhodes had also wrenched the shotgun from Jeanne's hand, and he was afraid he might have broken her finger with the trigger guard. He wasn't too sorry about it, however.

Vernell had dragged Jeanne down with her. Rhodes tossed the shotgun to Ruth and knelt down, straddling Jeanne. He untangled Vernell's hair from Jeanne's fingers while Jeanne writhed under him like a snake having a seizure. It wasn't easy, but he managed to keep her pinned.

When her hair was free, Vernell sat up and took a few deep breaths, all the while rubbing herself under the chin. Ruth Grady covered her with the shotgun, and the ambulance whined past, gravel spinning under its tires and lightbar flashing, headed for Quentin's place.

"You have some handcuffs?" Rhodes asked Ruth.

"Sure," Ruth said. "But who am I supposed to use them on?"

"This one," Rhodes said, nodding down at Jeanne. "You can put the gun away. She's not going anywhere."

Ruth lowered the shotgun and handed Rhodes a pair of plastic cuffs.

"Help me out," he said.

Ruth laid the shotgun down and took hold of one of Jeanne's arms that was trapped by Rhodes's knee. Rhodes slid back and grabbed the other arm. Jeanne thrashed and screamed, but Rhodes and Ruth got the cuffs on and drew them tight.

Rhodes stood up and looked over at Vernell, who was sitting on the grass, still rubbing under her chin and staring wide-eyed at Jeanne Arnot.

"You want to tell me what's going on?" Ruth said. "I thought we were going to arrest Vernell."

"Nobody was going to arrest Vernell," Rhodes said. "Ms. Arnot was going to kill her."

Vernell took a deep, gasping breath. Rhodes didn't blame her.

"Why?" Ruth asked.

"Because Ms. Arnot's the one who killed Henrietta and Terry Don Coslin. She was trying to put the blame on Vernell by claiming to be an eyewitness to Vernell's leaving Henrietta's room."

"I get it," Ruth said. "It's hard to contradict anyone when you've been killed while struggling with your captor."

"That's right," Rhodes said.

"But you didn't believe her," Ruth said.

"No. She might have been able to explain Henrietta, but she couldn't have explained Terry Don, and she couldn't have explained her missing whistle chain."

"Whistle chain?"

"Vernell borrowed the whistle," Jeanne said, talking fast from her awkward position on the ground. "She said she broke it. I don't know what happened to it."

"Nice try," Rhodes said. "But I don't believe you."

"A jury will believe me."

She sounded so convinced that Rhodes almost believed her himself.

"Believe you about what?" Ruth asked. "About the chain?"

"It's a long story," Rhodes said.

Jeanne Arnot changed her story later, after she had been a guest of Blacklin County for about ten hours in one of the few jail cells reserved for female prisoners. In Jeanne's new account, Terry Don was the one who had killed Henrietta. Jeanne claimed that she had no idea what they were arguing about but that she had opened the door just as Terry Don pushed Henrietta into the dresser. She said that she knew it was wrong to protect Terry Don, but he had cried and begged her.

"Terry Don and Henrietta shoulda locked the door to that room," Hack said.

"Is that what you and Miz McGee do?" Lawton asked. "Lock the door?"

Hack, Lawton, Rhodes, and Ruth Grady were sitting in the jail the morning after Jeanne Arnot's arrest, and Rhodes was in the middle of recounting his latest conversation with her. Hack didn't take kindly to Lawton's comments and started to get out of his chair, but Rhodes put up a hand and stopped him.

"I don't want you accidentally pushing Lawton into a desk," Rhodes told Hack. "We don't need any more customers in the cells right now."

"Well, then, he better watch his mouth is all I can say," Hack said.

Lawton tried to look contrite but without much success.

"It could've happened that way," Ruth Grady said, changing the subject.

"Could have," Rhodes said. "But it didn't."

"How does she explain Terry Don?" Ruth wanted to know.

"It wasn't just the begging and pleading. She also says that she loved him and that since it had been an accident, after all, she wasn't really doing anything wrong by protecting him. The part about the accident might even be true, but I don't think Terry Don did anything except run away. I think Ms. Arnot was jealous. She and Henrietta got into an argument over Terry Don, and that was that."

"I meant how does she explain killing Terry Don," Ruth said.

"Oh. Well, she says he asked her to meet him on the third floor of the college's main building to talk about things, and then he tried to kill her."

"That doesn't explain the whistle chain."

"She had a police whistle on a chain earlier," Rhodes said. "I saw it. Later it was on her key ring. Her story is that when Terry Don attacked her, she grabbed the whistle to call for help. They struggled, and he fell out the window."

"I hate to say this," Ruth said, "but that sounds pretty likely. Otherwise, why would she have had the whistle?"

"I think Terry Don threatened to turn her in," Rhodes said. "Or maybe he made some kind of demand about getting on book covers. Whatever he said, she got mad about it. There was another argument, and Terry Don got a little too physical. That's when she got out the whistle. Terry Don made a grab for it, she pushed him, and out the window he went. She hung on to the whistle, but he broke the chain, and it made that mark on his finger when it pulled out of his hand."

"So she didn't really kill anybody on purpose," Ruth said.

"That's her story," Rhodes said.

"And she's stickin' to it, I'll bet," Hack said. "I would if I was her. She might even get off if the jury believes her."

"It's going to be a little harder for her to explain why she tried to blow up the building with me in it, though," Rhodes said.

"I guess Hack forgot about the explosion," Lawton said.

"When you get to be his age, you start havin' little lapses like that."

"I'll lapse you," Hack said, starting to rise.

"Not here," Rhodes said, and Hack plopped back into his chair.

"What about the explosion?" Ruth asked.

"Ms. Arnot got back to the dorm and noticed that part of the chain was missing," Rhodes said. "She came back to look for it, and I was there, so she slugged me with the bucket." He touched the back of his head, which was still a little tender. "She couldn't find any of the chain, though, so she decided to get rid of all the evidence, if there was any. I just happened to be in the way."

"Lucky for you that old building has such high ceilings and lots of windows," Hack said. "That explosion could've been a whole lot worse."

"It was bad enough," Rhodes said. "It's going to take a lot of money to get the building back in shape."

"Do you think Chatterton will do it?" Ruth asked.

"I'm not sure. I'm going to see if maybe the historical societies won't pitch in and help. Maybe they can get a grant of some kind."

"They'll be lucky if they do."

"Speakin' of luck," Lawton said, "you were mighty lucky that Claude Appleby happened to be there."

"You won't get any argument from me about that," Rhodes said.

"Too bad he didn't see anything," Ruth said. "He might be the one who could convict Ms. Arnot for sure."

"Vernell will take care of that for us," Rhodes said. "She's our eyewitness. But Claude saw something, all right. He's just not talking. Yet."

"You think he will?"

"We'll see," Rhodes told her.

*   *   *

The Wal-Mart parking lot was crowded, but Rhodes managed to get a place right down front when a Ford Bronco pulled out just as he drove up. He parked and went inside, past the jewelry and the videos and the dog food, and found Claude in the sporting goods department.

"Time for your break?" he said.

Claude didn't look at all surprised to see Rhodes. It was almost as if he'd been expecting him.

"Let me get Eddie," he said.

They sat in the storeroom again, and Rhodes asked Claude why he hadn't told the whole truth the first time.

"I didn't think it would do any good," Claude said. "I didn't want to get anybody in trouble."

"She was already in trouble," Rhodes said.

"I know," Claude said, "but it was dark, and I couldn't see her face. I couldn't pick her out of a crowd for love or money."

"Just tell me what you saw, then."

"Well, I was out walking around. I wasn't looking in any windows or anything like that. I swear."

Rhodes nodded and said he believed him.

"I didn't see the man fall," Claude said. "I just heard it when the window broke. By the time I looked, he was already on the ground."

"But somebody came along."

"It was a woman," Claude said. "That's all I could tell. She bent down over him for a second, and that's all there was to it."

That must have been Jeanne, checking for pieces of the chain, Rhodes thought. He said, "You didn't go have a look?"

"After she left I did."

"But you didn't call me."

Claude looked at those interesting shoes of his.

"I should've, I guess. But I figured, what good would it do? The guy was dead, and I didn't know why or anything. For all I knew it was just an accident."

"You hung around for a while, though."

"Well, I saw you and Deputy Grady, so I knew something was going on. I guess you're glad I was there."

"I'm glad," Rhodes said. "I wish you'd seen who set the fire, though."

"I told you the truth about that part," Claude said.

"I'm glad to hear it," Rhodes said.

"Am I goin' to jail again?"

"I don't think so, Claude, but I do wish you'd learn to stay in your own house at night. If you don't, Billy Quentin's going to blow you apart with his shotgun one of these nights."

"He told me you'd confiscated it," Claude said. "Evidence."

"That's right. But he may get it back someday."

"He and I are sorta friends now," Claude said. "After I called that ambulance for him and all. And Grover already liked me."

Rhodes sighed. "Just stay home, Claude. Promise me."

"Yessir," Claude said.

As Rhodes was leaving the store, he stopped by the paperback rack. The writing workshop was over now, and he supposed all the writers, prepublished and otherwise, were home or heading in that direction. They'd have plenty of stories to tell, for sure.

He looked over the romance novels and spotted one by Serena Thayer. *Love's Wildest Hour.* There was a woman on the cover with long blond hair and a buckskin shirt, but she was secondary to the man, who was obviously Terry Don Coslin, who was holding her to his rock-hard pecs. His own fringed shirt was open to the navel, and his long hair was tossed by an invisible breeze. He was smiling confidently down into the woman's eyes, the way he'd smiled up at the stars behind Billy Quentin's house.

Rhodes took the book to the check-out stand to pay for it, and the cashier said, "That's Terry Don Coslin on that book cover. He was here in the store just the other day, and he signed a book for me." She put Rhodes's book in a plastic bag and handed it to him. "I just can't believe he's gone."

Rhodes took the bag. He thought about Terry Don and his great good looks, of all the book covers that he'd been on and of all the ones he'd posed for that were yet to appear.

"I think he'll be around for a while," Rhodes said.